Kentucky
Fried Crazy

Randall Stevens

ISBN: 9781979407953

Original editing by Tara Cohen

Vol. 2 Editing by Peter Gietl

Disclaimer: Some characters and events in this book are fictitious. Any similarity to real persons, living or dead, is coincidental and not intended by the author.

Tara –

Thanks for your encouragement and support in helping me turn this venture from a project into a book.

TABLE OF CONTENTS

Chapter 1

The day that changed my life was when I met the Beast...she called herself Betty, but she will always be the beast to me. One of my high school baseball teammates decided it would be nice to introduce her to me. I was new to the school and a junior at the time, and she had told my teammate Derek a few times that she wanted to meet me. He told her he would introduce us. Coming around the corner, she was standing in the lobby of the school. I had no idea who she was. Up to that point, I hadn't even seen her. And, as a teenage guy, I paid attention to all of the girls in high school. She looked older. Well, old to a high school kid like me. My first thought was that she was a teacher and that I just hadn't taken her class yet.

It was very interesting meeting the Beast for the first time; she would earn this awful nickname in spades down the road. It felt really strange because of how old she looked, but after being around her for a short time, it was obvious she had a big crush on me. It felt like I was a little fawn taking a drink out of a flowing brook in front of a hungry lion that hadn't eaten in weeks. I was definitely the prey, the meal she wanted to devour. She looked me up and down, taking every inch of me into her mind, and who knows what twisted thoughts and fantasies she had about us being together. It made me feel really uncomfortable. Cold chills started creeping up and down my back. The back of my shirt was sweaty, and I had an overwhelming nauseous churning in my stomach. I believed to my core that she was a teacher and didn't find out otherwise until two weeks had passed. At the time, I guess I didn't ask enough questions. It was an easy conclusion to come to that she was just a teacher who didn't mind fucking her students. Actually, she was the senior class president, and everybody loved her. So surprising that everyone loved her

5

as they did.

Betty was 5'7", average looking at best, thick to somewhat heavy and wore a lot of makeup, a *lot* of makeup. It was caked on and didn't flatter her one bit. Betty had shoulder length brunette hair and pale skin. She had shoulders like a linebacker and you could tell she was a force in regard to her physical strength. It was kind of scary knowing she was most likely quite a bit stronger than me at that time. She was definitely not my type at all.

After meeting her, she started showing up regularly at my baseball games. Without asking, she brought me McDonald's after my ball games. As a teenage kid, I was hungry all the time, so I thought this was cool. My ignorance and naivety caused me to not realize she had begun setting a trap. Very slowly and methodically she started weaving her dark web to ensnare me. Betty made no bones about it; she was interested in me. More than interested, an obsession began to take hold and grow within her. Attempting to quell her desires, I made it really obvious that I didn't think about her that way. Undeterred, Betty went about her way making subtle attempts to win me over. She showed up for every one of my baseball games, home or away. Often, my teammates and I would be on the bus traveling to away games and would spot her following behind in her parent's car.

She was also famous for driving through my neighborhood. The neighborhood crew would often notice a car slowly creeping by and knew exactly who it was. It was very strange having someone drive by so slowly just to get a glimpse of you. I hadn't yet put it together that she was stalking me. This detail would come back to haunt me later.

Chapter 2

My home life was pretty much a nightmare. My sister Gina and I relied on each other to make it through the day at home. My mother and her abusive boyfriend (one of many on the list of her abusive relationships) had things totally fucked up at our house. She thrived on finding every loser she could, and then somehow, convince them to move in with her. Our father lived in Massachusetts and we lived with him off and on when we were younger. We had been living with our mother for quite a while now.

My father was really intelligent and mostly a super nice guy, although somewhat pussy whipped by his second wife. We visited him during the summer up until I was a freshman in high school. My mother's newest love interest was a real fucking beauty. Asshole Bob would get drunk and beat on her, which in turn caused me to jump in and fight him. Bob was about six feet tall and 185 pounds or so. Depending on his level of inebriation, our altercations would go one of two ways; he would beat the shit out of me or I would get the better of him. This dickhead actually suggested to my mother that he should 'break in' my little sister so that it would be 'done right.' I couldn't fucking believe it. I had a baseball bat with his name on it and kept it close by, just in case I'd need to use it against this animal. The only feeling for my mother was disgust for allowing this creep into our home.

After spending a year in my neighborhood, where I had made numerous close friends, Bob and my mother decided to move us out to the country. This was the worst thing that could have happened to my sister and me. We moved into a run-down house that should have been condemned. Sometimes we would go without food for days, but Bob and Mom always had their beer, cigarettes, and pot to smoke. They never went without, and my resentment toward my mother and her asshole boyfriend grew by the day. This also allowed Bob to step up his abusive ways. We were living in the middle of nowhere, far from anyone. There was no one except my sister and me to hear our mother's screams or Bob's tirades. Every time I stepped into that house, I was angry. Bob had made a deal with the landlord that he would fix up the place if he wasn't charged rent. The place was an absolute dump. It only had electricity downstairs and no running water. We had to pull water from a cistern.

Without running water there were no working bathrooms, so we had to use an outhouse. This was the exact nightmare I'd pictured when my mother first brought up the idea that we were moving to Kentucky. I fucking hated my life out there and had to be ready for anything as soon as I walked through the door each and every day after school. Keeping vigil and keeping Bob away from my sister were my main focuses. My mother thrived on abuse; she was an abuse magnet, so to say. She would push people to do things they would never do. Bob was a complete asshole and abusive anyway. She didn't care as long as she could inflict pain on someone to get them to respond to her. One night, Bob had enough. All I heard coming from their bedroom were the moans and screams of my mother.

I'd finally reached my breaking point and was ready to kill Bob that night without regret. Grabbing my baseball bat, I waited outside their bedroom door for him to come out. I could hear my heart was pounding through my chest. It was so loud it was hard to concentrate. My hands clenched that baseball bat tightly and I felt the grooves of the wood on my fingers. I had every intention to take that bat to his head and hit him until he stopped moving and breathing. Adrenaline ran through me and feeling so pumped up, I knew that one hit might take his head completely off. He was going to die right there and then or be hurt so badly that he wouldn't hurt anybody ever again. There was no doubt he was going down.

Luckily for Bob, he never came out of the bedroom that night. I didn't have the stomach to walk in and lay into him in front of my mother. The sad part was the feeling that she would attack me and protect her fucking useless, pathetic excuse for a boyfriend, and I would probably be the one who ended up dead on the floor. It's terrible to know that your mother puts her loser boyfriends before her own children, but I knew deep down to my soul it was true. It was the one thing that kept me out of that bedroom.

That event really affected me. I decided from that night on, I wasn't going to take any more of his shit. I'd had enough and he had no idea what was in store for him. One night, my mother was already passed out drunk and couldn't have been woken by a nuclear explosion, and my sister was spending the night with one of her friends. Poor Bob had taken in quite a few cocktails, big mistake for him. For the first time ever, I picked a fight with him, calling him an asshole and telling him that he didn't mean shit to me. It was so empowering; he didn't have a chance against me that night. Having grown up fighting, all of my experience would come into play this one night. He came at me as expected. His right punch was telegraphed. I quickly stepped to the side and dodged it, then unleashed a right that stunned him. The force of the punch almost brought him to his knees right then and there. It was as though a caged animal had been set free. Tasting blood and liking it, I never let up. I hit him over and over, hearing the grunts come from his mouth, the breath escape from his lungs. Punches to the body followed up to the head. He kept moving backward, trying to escape, but there was no escape from my fury and anger that night. He fell into the staircase and I climbed on top of him. His face was beaten to a pulp from the flurry of punches rained upon him. Finally, it occurred to me that I was killing him. Not to mention, I was starting to get tired, so slowly I climbed off of him. He laid there barely moving, barely breathing. Feeling nothing, I made my way to the door and left the godforsaken house. I walked into town, not realizing how far I'd traveled. It was such a relief to not have to worry about my sister or my mother's abusive boyfriends anymore. That was the last time I set foot in that house.

Gina hated living in that situation in Kentucky and wanted to leave. She reached out to my grandparents and Aunt Jerry in California to see if they would mind her coming and staying with them for a while. They agreed, and our mother was smart enough not to try and prevent her from leaving. I didn't get to say goodbye to her, but it was such a relief knowing my sister would be safe. Bob eventually recovered from the beating I'd given him and decided to move to Lexington. My mother followed right along with him. I viewed her as the most pathetic excuse for a mother or human being, ever. It was shocking to see someone who was supposed to look out for you to be so weak and co-dependent on every single man she had ever encountered romantically.

Chapter 3

As my mother and Bob settled into their new love nest, I moved into my buddy Matt's house. Actually, his unfinished, dusty basement to be more precise. His parents didn't know, and we pulled it off for the entire summer without anyone discovering it. Matt was very good at keeping my living situation a secret. After his family finished eating he would sneak food down for me. His father, Stuart, was absolutely hilarious. Stuart and Matt were just alike, except for their ages. Stuart was gone all the time and was basically the town whore. He drove a van and we always saw him out with different women. Matt's mom, Julie, went to work and came home each day none the wiser of his behavior. It seemed that everyone knew about Stuart's antics except Julie; it was sad. Unfortunately, she tried to keep herself looking attractive by lying in the sun for hours at a time. Her skin was like leather where she had sunbathed entirely too much. Stuart still looked young and had a dynamic personality, while Julie began to show her age.

After a month, my mother suddenly showed up one day in the old neighborhood looking for me. Bob stayed in the car while she tried to convince me to move back in with them. There was no way I would allow myself to be exposed to that lifestyle again. Finally, I knew what it was like to be in a normal living situation after all those years of craziness. I'd rather have been in a foster home or simply run away. After some heated argument, she realized that I was no longer going to allow her to control my life. At this point, my resolve was unshakeable. She hadn't looked out for my sister or me for a long time and I could do a better job than she could.

Luckily, I stuck to my guns. As crazy as it may seem, within two weeks of our conversation about me going back to live with them, Bob lost his temper and snapped. He tied my mother up with extension cords. For two solid days, he tortured and beat on her relentlessly. Unfortunately, this time nobody was there to protect her and she took the brunt of his drunken anger. I was tired of being the responsible person in that crazy house. No matter what they did, she refused to see there were consequences to being with the men she chose. She had made her bed and now lain in it.

Shockingly, she finally did something after her last beat down from Bob. She went to the police and reported what he had done. Lexington's finest showed up and took Bob to jail. He finally got what he richly deserved. Later my mother tracked me down with the intention of convincing me to move with her to California, but I gave her the same response.

"Mom, I'm not coming with you to California; I'm getting ready to start my senior year of high school."

Taking responsibility for my own life, I was now on my own. It was pretty sad because she had two black eyes and looked pitiful. I loved my mother, but she had failed miserably as a parent.

The Michaels finally realized I was cohabitating in their basement. How long can one live in another's house without them knowing you have used the shower, bathroom and eaten their food for months? It was time for school to start back up for my senior year, anyway. Stuart and Julie asked me to come into the living room.

"Mark, tell us what is going on. Do you not have a place to live?"

Coming clean, I told them my mother had moved and I didn't have a place to go, but wanted to finish my last year of high school in Lawrenceburg.

They said I could stay, but that they needed to report the situation to family services. Within a few days, a counselor came and interviewed me. It was a tricky interview for a 16-year old kid to have and I worried I'd be placed into foster care when I just wanted to finish high school. To my amazement, Julie and Stuart allowed me to stay with them. Matt and his sister, Ariel, made room for me in their lives. Matt and I became like brothers with the same shared passion for young, teenage girls. His parents thought I might be a bad influence on him, but Matt was the most likely of us to be up to no good. We shared his room the entire year and had a great system. When one of us would sneak out to meet a girl we were pursuing, we would tie a string to the other's foot so we could wake them to let us in without getting caught. Our system was perfect and worked every time. Just typical teenage boys' antics.

One night, however, I woke up with my leg hanging out of the window. It was really late and Matt had been pulling on the string for a while, but I just wouldn't wake up. He'd been out enjoying himself with some young girl. We fed off each other like that. He had a very dynamic, engaging personality that drew in the girls. I was the new guy and had that going for me, especially with my Massachusetts accent. The Kentucky girls knew I was from elsewhere and it helped me land them in school.

I met a girl named Laura and we became super-close friends and had really hot chemistry. One night she was housesitting at a friend's place overnight and wanted me to come stay with her. We had an incredible closeness that was hard to describe. She met me at the door and I knew things were going to be different this night, there was electricity in the air. Walking in the door we attacked each other, completely oblivious to anything else in the world. We kissed deeply and passionately like our lives depended on it. We got to the bed and had amazing sex all night long, with the stamina only teenagers posses. The pure lust and passion were almost too much for me to handle at the time. It was an unbelievable experience. I hadn't felt so much passion or desire for someone ever before.

Using our string system, I got back into the house. One night, Matt and I decided we needed to get out and chase girls, so we decided to sneak out after everyone went to bed. Matt jumped into the driver's seat of Stuart's van and I pushed it down the street so we could cruise around. We didn't start it until we were way out of hearing distance of the house. It was a rush. We felt like we were getting away with murder. We were exhausted from pushing that heavy-ass van down the road but had a great time that night. Matt and I were not shy when it came to talking to girls, though the most action we usually got was kissing a chick or playing with her boobs. It was amazing how many girls beeped at us riding in Stuart's van. We knew we were busted. People kept asking Stuart why he didn't stop and say hello when he was out cruising. It didn't take him too long to figure out that Matt and I had heisted his van. He didn't throw too much of a fit, but we were definitely reprimanded for our actions. It was quite interesting that Stuart knew so many people in Lawrenceburg.

One of our adventures out with the van led to us getting lucky with some older, married women. By older, I mcan they were Kentucky older...21 or 22. They were bored girls who'd married their high-school sweethearts who worked the night shift. They decided to flirt and play around with some high school boys. I was super paranoid, feeling that Betty was always watching me and had spies reporting back to her, though we weren't dating. It was amazing

how many times I'd do something, and it somehow got back to the Beast. The girl who was the boldest and hottest for me let me know that she was definitely down to fuck. Even as a dumb teenager I was able to figure it out and knew it was going to happen. Matt wasn't too impressed with the other girl he was entertaining and bailed on me. Staying with Lindsey and Sarah, we rode around for a while. In my mind, I was hoping that these girls would invite me back to someone's house and we would all end up naked, but that was not the case.

Lindsey marked her territory and was the only one who would hook up with me that night. She dropped Sarah off and asked if I'd like a ride home. Of course, this was bullshit.

"Is that what you want," I asked her.

She commented that she never had done this before, but I seriously doubted that. Lindsey asked if I'd come home with her and have a cocktail. Jumping at the chance, the next thing I knew we were walking into her apartment that was within a half a mile of the high school. I was so eager and started grabbing at her bra as we kissed. She slowed me down and said to be patient; it would happen. In what felt like forever to me, we finally made it to her bedroom. I felt no guilt or remorse for this married woman 'taking advantage' of me. In my mind, because she was older, the decision she made had to be ok.

Being 16, I could have sex over and over and it absolutely rocked her world. I was able to go longer and longer without running out of energy. She told me I fucked like a porn star and that she was worried she might become addicted. After we finished, I walked home so she wouldn't know where I lived. For the next few weeks she called me constantly, which was tempting, but I knew that by going down that path, it could end up with her husband and myself meeting in an ugly confrontation. With everything going on in my life, that was the last thing I needed.

Julie was uptight all the time. She had to be somewhat miserable being married to Stuart, who was gone all the time, but accepted this as her life. She knew in her heart that he was out banging other women, but stayed in denial. It was easy to imagine this caused a lot of sexual frustration, too. She'd lie outside during the summer, lathered up with baby oil, trying to get tan to look good, not realizing the result was like a leather suitcase. Julie resolved herself to the fact that her life was about raising kids and nothing more. She was super nice, and I felt really bad that she lived in that situation, but she accepted Stuart as her husband and dealt with the consequences. It's hard to imagine the things that went on in the back of Stuart's van.

One condition for staying with the Michaels was that I had to go to church each week. Not being religious at all, it was hard for me to care about church, but since the Michaels had sacrificed a lot by allowing me staying with them, I agreed. Each week was the same routine on Sunday. It seemed a ridiculous practice, going to church each and every week. As hard as I tried, I never got anything out of it. The people seemed like mindless cattle without thoughts or minds of their own. It was just something I needed to do to live with the Michaels. This was fine until one week when the preacher gave a sermon I just couldn't swallow.

Not having gone to church growing up, I wasn't housebroken in that setting. I'd been a cocky kid who always stood up for himself and didn't know when to let things lie. Hell, I had a 17-year- old's brain that was not too evolved, to say the least. The preacher gave his sermon, words spewing from his lips, striking a chord with me in a bad way. After droning on and on, he finished with a threat.

"If you have not been baptized by this church, each and every one of you will go to hell

when you die!"

For some reason, this really got my attention and I found his statements ridiculous. Something inspired me to address his comments. Julie's face looked worried as I stood up, but I just couldn't help it. I'd tried hard not to cause any problems since moving in with them. Being a 17-year-old punk, I stood in front of the whole congregation and challenged him.

"So, you're telling me that if I haven't been baptized in this church, I'm going straight to hell if I walk out of here and get hit by a car?"

"Yes, that's right," he responded.

"Then why in the hell am I sitting here listening to you and wasting my time unless I've been doused in your holy water?"

Julie was absolutely horrified. She knew that even though I was compliant, I'd never adopt the doctrine and become religious. After that, they didn't ask me to go to church again. The premise of organized religion was always a mystery to me and this event solidified how ridiculous it was. Each church believes they are right and that every other church or religion is wrong. How can everyone be right and wrong at the same time? So ridiculous.

Chapter 4

Meanwhile Betty was spinning the web in which she planned on ensnaring me. She was passive at first, trying to get my attention, but then things heated up.

She began showing up in my neighborhood for no reason. I talked to her, feeling obligated because of how nice she had been to me. She did a lot of nice things for me. Really, she had become the mother figure in my life and she knew it. Betty used this to her advantage and started digging in to control me.

Betty also carried a 4.0 GPA in high school. She had a full ride to college and numerous scholarships that would pay every financial obligation she would encounter in her four years of undergrad work. As class president, she was front and center at the senior class' graduation and gave a speech. As the principal called her name to receive a diploma, it took what felt like a half hour to list off all of the scholarships and grants she had received. I was amazed at her scholastic accomplishments.

When they say girls mature at a much faster rate than boys, this is no joke. Especially if you run across someone who is flat out manipulative and incredibly intelligent at the same time. They can and will have their way with you and you won't even know what happened.

During the summer before my senior year, I felt vulnerable and Betty sensed it. She pounced at the chance to get me while I was down and confused about my plans after graduation. She had been giving me rides and taking me out. I hadn't asked for any of it, but I didn't say no either. Eventually, I started to wear down and feel the pressure of her calculated obsession.

There was such an immense feeling of burden and I had no idea why. After a while, a switch went off and dating felt obligatory because she had made it so clear this was what she wanted. This seemed kind of crazy since I had expressed to her, in no uncertain terms, that I didn't think of her in that way. There was no attraction to her, but I felt the pressure mounting and didn't realize she had set this up from the start. I fell right in line and, eventually she finally had me. How could this have happened? It makes sense, in retrospect, how female teachers can seduce their students and completely control them. This is exactly how I felt. This relationship was not wanted, but there was no way out either. As soon as people realized we had started dating, other girls stopped speaking to me. Everyone in school was very afraid of the Beast and I had no idea why. They obviously knew something I didn't, and damn them, nobody told me.

Completely oblivious, I didn't realize that her younger sister Melissa was interested in dating me as well. The Beast quickly put a stop to that, though I considered Melissa cute and would have liked to date her. The word was out and I could no longer have fun. Our first kiss was awful and every kiss from then on was on the verge of nauseating. It's so hard to describe the feeling of kissing someone you have no attraction to. Kissing your sister comes to mind. How did I let myself get cornered like this? After a while, I developed a routine dating the Beast aka Betty. It was total numbness; no feelings, emotions or love, whatsoever. She set the agenda on everything that we did while my friends sat back, stunned, watching me fall into line doing everything she wanted.

Once senior year started, every weekend, like clockwork, she borrowed her friend's car and drove to see me from college. Sometimes during the week, she just showed up unexpectedly.

Not having any money, she always took us out and paid for everything. She took control without me realizing the repercussions. Each time I saw her, darkness filled my heart more and more. Even at this early stage, I began to despise her. She was just so happy to date me, like having a shiny new toy, and all she wanted was to show me off to everyone. Being fairly cute in high school, but no supermodel, I couldn't understand it. She developed a fixation on me and I was too stupid to realize it.

Eventually, as any normal teenager who didn't like who he was dating, my eyes began to wander, checking out other girls. For some reason, I couldn't just pull the trigger on Betty and cut her off. My rebellion began by making it known that I was available, though clearly this was not the case. The girls I was interested in always said, 'I thought you are dating Betty,' and I'd tell them that I really didn't care too much for her and that we were going to break up. That would typically suffice until word got out to Betty and then somehow, someway, she would get the word back to the girl that a hands-off policy was in full effect, or they would pay. There was nowhere to escape to in that small town.

No matter how many times I tried to break up with her, she just wouldn't allow it. Betty was relentless. Someone would tell her that I'd been out with other girls, and I'd admit to messing around, but she didn't care and wanted to work it out and still date. The prophetic nature of that situation wouldn't hit me until later.

Things went on like this for a while with me messing around, her finding out and wanting to talk it over and stay together. Being so emotionally weak at that time, I just didn't have the balls to end the relationship. On numerous occasions, I'd done things that no girl in their right mind would put up with, such as cheating on her without regard for getting caught. Betty put up with it, no matter what.

Talking with my best friends from high school, Rob and Jenna, about Betty all the time, Jenna never understood why I went out with her in the first place, though she didn't voice her feelings to me. We grew extremely close spending every day of our senior year together in art class. The art teacher was in his last year before retirement and just didn't give a fuck about us doing any art projects. This was fine by my friends and me. We spent all our time talking about life, Jenna's boyfriend, Jimmy, and everything that Rob was going through. He had a very interesting lifestyle. His dad was involved with a younger, attractive woman named Allison who was not much of a mom to Rob or his younger sister, Caroline.

Rob's dad, also named Robert, always gave him ridiculous chores to do before he was allowed to come out and play with the kids in the neighborhood. For example, Rob would have to dig up a number of rocks in his front yard and put them in a wheelbarrow. Sometimes I'd help so he could get out faster and enjoy his time playing ball with the guys, but I began to realize that it was just a way to control him and keep him busy at all times, as Robert's girlfriend Allison wanted. It was hard to tell what her motivation was, but she had interesting ways of controlling Rob's dad. She was hot, so that played a factor in the dumb shit he made his son do. Having a penis sucks sometimes.

I'd been attracted to Jenna for some time, but never let her know back in art class. She had been in a long-term relationship with Jimmy for over two years, although they hadn't even slept together. There was no way I could understand that concept. She gave us the details on how and why they had never slept together. For some reason, she actually thought that sex would be a life-changing event and like most high school girls, wanted to wait for the right opportunity. Rob and I encouraged her every day to get it over with, but she had developed a routine with

Jimmy and wouldn't give up the goods. The funny thing was that she broke up with Jimmy and started dating an older guy who her father knew because they were both firemen. She lost her virginity to this guy almost instantly. I'm not sure why, but that absolutely bothered me. Maybe it was the fact that she had been in a relationship for two years and the poor guy never got any release, or that I didn't get the chance to deflower her.

As senior year progressed, I finally saw light at the end of the tunnel. Surely, this would be the end of my relationship with Betty. Graduation was coming, and I'd have to move to California with my Grandparents because I didn't have money or a place to stay in Kentucky. No way could we carry on a long-distance relationship like that. It was such a relief to not have to be the bad guy and end the relationship because I didn't want her; circumstances would break us up instead. She had a full scholarship to Georgetown College in Kentucky and I didn't have a place to live. This would be easy, right? Wrong.

"It's too bad you can't come with me, you're in school with scholarships and your family is here," I stupidly said,

"I love you Mark; I'll quit school and come with you," she immediately replied.

"Betty, you have a full ride to college, an opportunity few people get. You can't just throw it away."

Nobody should throw away the scholarships she was getting and had worked her whole life for, for somebody who cheated and tried to break up with her numerous times. No sane person would ever do that.

Betty was obsessed with me and I hadn't realized it. That's when it hit me like a sledgehammer. My pulse raced as she talked craziness about coming with me to California. A massive pit grew in my stomach and cold sweat ran down my back. Darkness crept into my life.

Desperately, I tried to stop her from quitting school, which would have been a huge mistake for both of us. My efforts went as far as to show up at her parents' house and speak with them about her radical plans, trying to get them to intervene and talk some sense into her. She went her whole life setting goals and trying to get into college. I just couldn't wrap my head around it. Her parents did their best to talk her out of it, but she wouldn't be swayed. What really needed to happen was for me to step up and tell her I didn't want her to come with me. Unfortunately, I was an emotional pussy at that time. Getting more than a little scared now, I never had dealt with anything like this in my life and didn't know how to handle it. What on earth would possess somebody to throw their life away on some kid with no plans for the future and no money?

She set the ball in motion and quit school. The immense feeling of guilt about her throwing such an opportunity away really fucked me up; I didn't know how to feel or react. There seemed to be no other option than to let her come with me to California. An enormous pit grew in my stomach; I felt sick. How could I get out of this? Over and over, I'd thought of every angle to get out of it, but failed to just do the simple, straight forward thing: simply tell her I didn't love her and didn't want to be with her. The solution was so simple, but I just couldn't bring myself to do the one thing that would stop the craziness. The only thing left to do was accept the fact that she was coming to California with me.

After graduating and expressing my immense gratitude to the Michaels, it was time to move. The experience I had with Stuart, Julie, Matt, and Ariel was life-changing. Never before had I'd been in a situation that was so normal and stable. It really hit home to me and allowed me to flourish during my last year of high school. My mother still helped me out sometimes and bought me a plane ticket to San Francisco right after graduation and I left my life in Kentucky. It

was hard saying goodbye to the friends I'd grown so close to in school. The one thing I wanted to leave behind, unfortunately, was the one and only thing I brought with me to California.

Betty was going to follow me on a Greyhound bus. My mother wasn't about to buy a stranger a plane ticket. Getting there first, I'd had a week to myself before the Beast arrived. It was great to catch up with my cousins, grandparents, aunts, uncles and my sister Gina. My mother had shacked up with an old boyfriend. While I didn't understand the history between my mother and this deadbeat, he was really tiny and I wasn't concerned about having physical altercations with him. Apparently, my mother's boyfriend owned the house they stayed in. We moved in and everything was fine at the beginning.

Chapter 5

As soon as Betty arrived, my mother made it known that she didn't care for her. Right from the go, she made it uncomfortable. It was probably the worst thing she could have done. The most twisted part is that my mother got so ugly that I was forced to stand up for the Beast. How could I have ended up defending this person who I couldn't stand? It made me sick to my stomach, but I really felt guilty. My mother was hard on people; I'd grown up seeing her bash friends and family members. There was no doubt that she was bipolar and undiagnosed. She was the black sheep of the family and had been ostracized for quite a long time.

It was crazy standing up for Betty, but guilt can make you do crazy things. The more my mother dug in and made life uncomfortable, the more I shielded the Beast. How ironic; I had envisioned California as my salvation from her, but it turned into the place where she would sink her hooks into me even tighter.

Things became so uncomfortable at my mother's house that we moved out. Knowing what she was capable of, I felt sorry for the Beast for the last time ever. We looked for a new place and moved into a one-bedroom apartment. It was tiny, but that didn't matter; it was the first place I could take responsibility for and call home. We lived right off of El Camino Real on the peninsula south of San Francisco and it wasn't too bad for an apartment. It was close to my family and it was comfortable.

The Beast took a job at a high-risk loan company, the kind of place that charges loan shark rates, legally, for people who can't afford a loan in the first place. My grandfather 'Pop' got me a job at the Cow Palace where they held the National Rodeo Championships. It was mostly used for concerts when I began working there with my cousins. There was only work a couple of times a week because they didn't alwayshave events going on.

It allowed me to make decent money for a 17-year-old kid. With my cousins, Dan and Gib, we devised a way to make extra money while working certain concerts. Our job was to direct traffic to the parking lots to allowthe cars to park in an orderly fashion. Whenever possible, we would block off thirty spots in front of the concert hall and wait for people with too much money and no patience to approach us in their cars. I could always tell when someone was going to ask me about those special spots. They would say something like, "Hey, I want to go park down front where the cones are. How do I do that?" I would direct them to my cousin Dan and told the customer to give him $20 dollars, and the spot was his. Most people laughed and said no problem at our side business endeavor. We usually split four to six hundred dollars between us, depending upon the concert.

It was pretty cool working at a concert venue. We got to go into concerts for free and go straight to the front of the stage wearing our Cow Palace jackets. We actually got to meet Eddie Money and saw a number of acts that were popular during the time. The Scorpions, Prince and Night Ranger were a few acts we witnessed. It was fun working with my grandfather and cousins. Dan and Gib took full advantage of working at the Cow Palace. They would jump into a car in a second to get stoned with the concert fans. Once they went three hours without being seen as we were preparing for a concert that evening. We started working at 10 a.m.. and the concert started at 7 p.m.

My life went on this way for a while in California. Most of the time, I did everything in my power to make excuses to spend time with my family, play softball with my cousins, and just act like the teenager I was. Betty was not fond of my behavior, but couldn't do anything about it. I'd find any excuse to avoid being with her. By this time, the sight of her utterly revolted me.

One Saturday morning I woke up hungover from being out with my cousins and partying a little too hard. The Beast was gone, as she worked most Saturdays. There was a knock at the door. Deciding to ignore it, I tried to go back to sleep. My head pounded, but there were no pain meds to help. Knock, knock, knock, it went again with more force. Whoever was knocking knew I was home. Wearing a holey, and I mean holey pair of tighty-whities and grizzly bear slippers, I made my way to the door. My head throbbed with each step; my pulse was pounding on the sides of my temples. Thank god my apartment was dark.

Reaching for the door, I turned the knob and barely opened it to see who the hell was trying to torture me on a Saturday morning. Peaking my head around the corner, an entire family was standing in front of my doorway. Completely confused and wondering what they were doing at my door, I tried to assess their agenda, but couldn't. The man was in a three-piece suit with his son, who was probably ten years old. His wife and daughter, who was about eight or so, were in very lovely dresses that fell below the kneecaps. Confused as to why they were knocking on my door, I asked, "Can I help you?"

Immediately, the husband introduced himself and his family and asked, "Do you have a relationship with God?"

This can't be happening to me, I thought. All they could see was my face; the rest of me was protected behind the door in an NC-17 state. As nicely as possible, I told him it wasn't a good time now and that they would be welcome to come back at another time. He was all too ready for that kind of response and told me that he wanted to come in and have a quick conversation about the Lord. Beginning to lose my patience and growing more agitated, constant rebuttals flowed from his mouth. It felt like he was the best used car salesman of all time and I had no idea how to (politely) make him go away. My temper started to come out and I finally told him I wasn't going to let them in and was shutting the door. Right at that moment, quick like a ninja, he placed his foot firmly in my doorway. This was obviously a technique that had been practiced numerous times. Surely they were used to doors being closed on them. Instantly, I saw red; my head throbbed and this fucking asshole wouldn't let up. Looking him straight in the eye, I gazed over at his wife and we made immediate eye contact. Anger took over as I pulled opened my apartment door fully exposing my cock and balls to his lovely wife and children. They got the full monty as my underwear didn't cover much. "Come on in! Let's have a fucking conversation about God!"

His wife's eyes opened like a deer in headlights; she was in complete shock to see another man's junk laid out so openly in front of her. Never mind the poor kids who had been exposed to that. He finally conceded, "Oh, it's not a good time right now."

"No shit," was all I could say.

They quickly scampered away and allowed me to get back into bed with my headache that was now ten times worse. The fanatic God family had pushed my blood pressure up to the max. I'm sure they won't soon forget the visit they had with me.

Life went on for a while; I lived with the Beast and found as many excuses as possible to spend as much time away from her as I could. My main problem was that of feeling controlled by her. I'm sure that she thought she loved me. I just wanted freedom, but felt jailed with her up my ass all the time. Desperately I tried to spend time away from her, to have some semblance of a teenage guy's normal life, but she wouldn't let it happen. It drove me crazy. Her control starting to take hold of every aspect of my life. It was getting to the point that something had to be done; I couldn't live like this anymore.

Chapter 6

Numerous things were done to keep myself occupied while trying to figure out what I was going to do with my life. I met and developed a crush on my barber, Sherry. She was very attractive with short, dark hair and an absolutely fantastic body. Sherry had a beautiful smile and an amazing habit of pressing her breast against my shoulders while she cut my hair. Whew, I was so hot for her and grateful to have a smock on at the time to hide my raging hard on. It was always a challenge getting out of that chair without having her notice my stiffy. She must have known what she was doing to me and I definitely think she liked me. Each time I got a haircut, she took more and more time pressing her body against me. Betty always commented about how awfully short my hair was and asked why I got it cut all the time. If I'd had any balls, I'd have asked Sherry out, but being chained to the Beast prevented this. On this fateful day, I would meet someone else who would change the course of my life forever.

Leaving the shop, I took a right and started making my way to the bus stop to catch a ride back to my apartment. A white van drove by, made a U-turn and headed back my way. For some reason, I knew it had turned around for me, but didn't know why. As it passed me, it slowed down and pulled over to the curb. A large, tall, black man got out of the van, dressed in the sharpest military uniform I had ever seen. Slowly, he walked around the front of the van in a manner that was impressive. He seemed to glide effortlessly, precisely, with every movement. "Hey son, do you need a ride somewhere?" I was surprised that he had stopped and bothered to ask if I needed a ride.

This guy was in a U.S. Marine Corps dress blue uniform, which projected something awesome. I was so impressed looking at him, the uniform, ribbons, shiny medals and manner in which he carried himself. I'd always been impressed with the Marine Corps and knew they were the most elite fighting force in the world. Contemplating taking the bus and sitting next to some loser, I quickly answered, "Sure, I'll take a ride." He happened to be a recruiter. He had found the perfect candidate who was vulnerable and looking for a way out of a mundane life; within 30 minutes I had joined the Marine Corps.

As we rode in his van we talked about my life and plans for the future. I wanted more, to not be stuck in this go-nowhere lifestyle. He was really smart and picked up on my pain and anguish, stuck without any real hope for the future with Betty in my life. The Marine Corps sounded so amazing and I bought all of it, hook, line, and sinker. Within the first five minutes of our conversation, I'd been sold on the opportunity and was all in.

The main thing running through my head was a chance to be free from the Beast. It was motivation like I had not felt in such a long time; it was my ticket out of this mess! The recruiter must have told this story to his fellow recruiters and had a big laugh. He basically picked someone up off the street and got them to commit to the Marine Corps. It was amazing how excited I was about my decision. It was as if someone had been looking out for me and made me meet this guy, Sgt Davis. I'd desperately wanted to go to college, but had no money. Sgt Davis told me the Marine Corps would help with that, with the GI Bill. And the best part, Betty couldn't follow me into the military. This was an unequivocal fact. Being in the delayed entry program, I'd have to wait it out for three months. Finally, I was going to be rid of her.

Entering the door to our apartment, it felt like I was walking on air. Betty saw my face and knew something was up. "Betty, I just joined the Marine Corps." The look of pure shock and

horror came over her face. I reveled in telling her that I'd made my own decision and there was nothing she could do about it, no argument she could make as to the bad reasons for joining the military. It was going to give me the money to go to college and get me away from the living nightmare of having her in my life. She was exceptionally distressed and knew that deep down she was going to lose me. The gravity of what I'd just committed myself to and her loss of control over me was coming to an end. It was such a relief. Betty finally accepted that I had joined the military, and her mind started plotting the next move to keep me in her trap.

Chapter 7

About a month before I was supposed to leave for boot camp, Betty got a distressing call about her sister. Her mother was in an absolute panic. Betty's sister, Melissa, had just given birth. Somehow, nobody knew she was pregnant, right up until that day. Melissa kept the pregnancy a secret while going to school and no one noticed that she had gained weight. She went into labor right at school and was rushed to the hospital. When she gave birth, her mother and father were in complete shock. Betty's family was one of the most repressed families I've ever met. Religious guilt was placed on the kids the whole time they grew up and this drove all of their decisions. After Melissa had the baby, she came up with an amazing story to explain how she had gotten pregnant. Her story was incredulous and "out there" in regard to believable facts. At the time, everyone felt exceptionally sorry for her.

She said that she'd been gang-raped by five black guys at the high school Sweet Sixteen tournament in Lexington, KY. They had surrounded her in the hallway of her hotel and dragged her into a guest room. They took turns raping her over and over. The whole thing made me sick to my stomach. Being very fond of Melissa, a range of emotions went through me from anger to shock to absolute sadness at what these gangsters had done this to this poor, innocent girl.

Betty convinced me that she needed to return to Kentucky and asked me to come with her. Somehow, Melissa's baby came out completely milk white; a bit strange since she had allegedly been raped by a number of black guys. She immediately gave the baby up for adoption. Of course, I saw pictures and the story just didn't add up. I'd heard from some of my friends that she had messed around with a guy from high school about nine months ago. She stuck to her story though and never admitted to anything else. After an initial investigation, with no witnesses or any video from the hotel corroborating her story, the police knew the story was bogus and dropped the investigation within a week. Nothing about her story added up and she couldn't remember the details the same each time.

Melissa really wanted Betty to come home to Kentucky and that was fine with me since I was on borrowed time, waiting to go to boot camp. She got herself transferred from her loan-sharking job to a store in northern Kentucky. We didn't have many possessions, so we sold the car and she flew to Kentucky. Not wanting to fly with her, I made an excuse for her to go take care of her sister and said I'd catch up with her later.

I should have used that time to break it off with her while she was out of state, but honestly, I missed the friends that I hadn't seen in a year and decided to head to Kentucky. It was nice to visit them. My best friend, Rob, was in college and struggling pretty badly. His father, Robert, made a lot of money but didn't give him much financial support to help him get through school. The worst part was that because his father made good money, it counted against Rob for getting scholarships and grants. Unfortunately, Rob's father held on to his money with an iron grip and Rob had nothing to eat, but Ramen noodles. Everybody has to suck it up while they are in college and tighten their belts, but this was ridiculous. He was practically starving.

Rob was enrolled at Eastern Kentucky in a serious

party town. Betty kept busy between spending time with her sister and working in Covington, near Cincinnati. Rob and I hung out and partied like rock stars; it was an absolute blast. Betty was so preoccupied, she actually let me enjoy some freedom. After meeting some really fun, attractive college girls, I knew that I'd been missing out by being anchored down by the Beast. After hanging out with Rob for a few days, I spoke with him about my decision to join the Marines.

After assessing his situation at college, I thought it would be better for him to come with me and join the Marine Corps, and wouldn't you know it, he decided to join me. I'm sure he realized that if he kept going the way he was at school, he probably wasn't going to graduate anyway, so why not go along with your best friend?

I moved into Betty's small apartment in Covington and got a job at Captain D's, a fast food fish place. Every shift was spent frying fish and french fries. It was the kind of job where you realized that anything would be better than working at a fast food restaurant. The nice thing was that it was within walking distance of the apartment and I worked with a few attractive girls. Betty did her thing while a great deal of my time was spent getting ready for the Marine Corps. Every day I ran farther and farther, trying to get myself ready for what the Marines would put me through. There was a tree right next to the apartment building on which I would do pull-ups. At first, I could only do a couple, but kept my eye on the prize, knowing that I'd be pushing my body to the limit soon enough. After a month I was doing 20 pull-ups.

We always invited Rob up to stay with us and eventually, when it got closer to the time when we would report to boot camp, he moved in with us. Rob and I worked out and ran every day; we had no idea what was in store for us. Trying to distance myself from Betty, I knew what entering the military would mean for our relationship. Luckily, she had a lot on her plate worrying about her family issues, so she would go to Lawrenceburg a few times a week, usually on the weekends. Meanwhile, a great deal of my time was spent flirting with and sometimes making out with the girls who worked with me at Captain D's.

When it finally came time for me to give notice and let my manager know I was going into the Marines, he said, "I had you tagged for an assistant manager role" It was priceless. Thankfully, I now knew my destiny would not be slinging battered fish into a massive pool of hot grease.

Chapter 8

On May 27, 1986, I said what felt like my last goodbye to Betty. It was so liberating to leave her and know it was finally over, our sham of a relationship. Betty dropped Rob and me off at the Military Entrance Processing Station (MEPS) in Cincinnati. The MEPS station is where they prescreen you before sending you to boot camp. They give you a physical and have you sign the final paperwork. I was given a key to a room at a Holiday Inn and waited for our flight the next day. Rob and I spent that evening walking around Cincinnati exploring the city. He commented that we should eat at a fancy restaurant that we had passed. At that moment, it occurred to me that I had never been to an expensive restaurant that I had paid for in my life. Neither of us got much sleep that entire night from the stress and anxiety of what was ahead of us.

The next morning, a shuttle van took us to the airport and we began our journey to Parris Island, South Carolina. We talked a little but soon grew quiet. Fear and uncertainty consumed us.

Loading onto the plane, a knot formed in my stomach forcing me to relax and breathe. The Marine Corps has a systematic and psychological way of completely messing with your mind when you first reach Parris Island. Rob and I said nothing to each other as the plane began its descent. We were deep in our own thoughts, getting mentally prepared.

After getting off the plane, we loaded onto a Greyhound bus that made its way on a dark, deserted route for what seemed like hours. The bus took turn after turn in pitch-black darkness. We had no idea where the hell we were or where we were going. Not knowing where you are headed makes you that much more anxious. As much as I wanted to control my emotions, my pulse raced.

Anxiety pulsed from everyone on the bus. Each and every face was filled with fear as our bus arrived on the island around midnight. You could have heard a pin drop; nobody murmured a word. When the bus finally stopped, we heard the air brakes release with a 'whoosh' sound. The next second, a scary DI (drill instructor) flew violently up the stairs of the bus.

"You have ten seconds to get off this bus and get on the yellow footprints!"

People jumped through their asses to get off that bus! We scrambled to line up on the painted, yellow footprints in front of the barracks in a platoon formation, like a military formation for civilian idiots.

"Get on line! Eyes front!" they barked over and over. We were all stunned and traumatized.

The DIs kept us up all night and the entire next day, trying to break us mentally right from the start. We spent the night mostly in silence. All night long we were on our feet, checking in one by one to sign paperwork and be issued all of our gear which would stay with us for the entire four years we would spend in the Marine Corps. This was by far the most exhausted I'd ever been in my life. Each of us tried to keep it together as we waited for that first night of sleep. Feeling dead on my feet as my head hit the pillow, I instantly fell asleep.

The next day, we marched to the barbershop and got our heads scalped. The barbers who gave these so-called 'haircuts' had been doing this for years. They actually drew blood from your scalp, as they pressed down hard to remove each hair. It lasted maybe 30 seconds at the most, but afterward, you could feel your head throbbing.

Most people think boot camp is just grueling physical torture, which in a large sense it is. The true nature of Marine Corps boot camp is to psychologically break you down and build you back up in the Marine Corp image. You spend the first couple of days sitting Indian style with your left leg over your right, left hand on left knee and right hand on right knee. Sitting like this, for a man who isn't used to sitting this way, can be really uncomfortable as you begin stretching out your leg muscles. We all lined up with our shirts off and walked between the Navy nurses. Each one had a large immunization gun that fired inoculations into our arms from both sides. It felt like we were being hit in the arm by NFL linebackers from both sides as the needles penetrated our skin repeatedly.

There is a reason for every single thing you do in boot camp though you may not figure it out till the end. You always sat in some kind of formation. Everywhere you went you were herded around like cattle. Cattle walking in unison, that is. Everything was structured as we were issued uniforms, issued Marine Corps gear, took a piss test and sat around waiting.

Sitting in formation, lined up directly behind another recruit, I waited to be called up to sign some paperwork. For some reason my eyes were not trained perfectly on the guy's head directly in front of me. You are not allowed to look around while in boot camp and I paid a price for taking my eyes off of the head in front of me. The DI caught me looking at him. He flew down through the seated recruits until he was right upon me.

"Get your eyeballs off me, RECRUIT!"

It absolutely scared the shit out of me as he yelled at me for a while. Eventually, I said, "Yes sir, no sir," enough times to pacify him to leave me alone.

We waited for enough recruits to arrive in order to form a training platoon. The day finally arrived when we received word that we would meet our drill instructors and begin real boot camp. Our training platoon mustered outside and we marched over to the squad bay to meet the DIs. This is where we were going to spend the next three months training to become Marines. My platoon entered the barracks and sat in formation in rows of eight back, nine deep. The captain in charge of our training battalion came out to give us instructions and welcome us to boot camp. He gave us some words of encouragement, told us that we made a big decision and that he was proud of us for taking the step we had. I saw Rob from the corner of my eye. We really hadn't been able to even have a conversation for the past four days since arriving. Starting to feel pretty good, I took a breath. I'd barely breathed or said one word the past four days since arriving at Parris Island. In the slightest way, I let my guard down after the captain gave such a great speech about joining the brotherhood of fellow Marines.

"I'd like to introduce you to your drill instructors," the captain said.

Just then, the doors opened and in came three badass drill instructors with uniforms crisply pressed, every medal and ribbon beaming off them. Their shoes mirrored like glass, shining a high gloss. Every movement was precise. You could hear the clicking of their heels hitting the deck at exactly the same time, each and every time. It was perfection and the kind of precision I had never experienced in my life. They marched in, did a left face and saluted the captain. The captain saluted back and they moved back into parade rest, standing in front of my platoon.

"At this time, your drill instructors will give the Drill Instructor Oath," the captain told us.

If you heard it, it would make you feel pretty good about their job and what they were going to do for you. Soft and fluffy statements like, "We promise to help motivate you to perform to the best of your abilities," and, "We will help guide you and support your transition into becoming

Marines." The bullshit that rolled out of their mouths made me drop my guard and relax for a minute. *Oh, it's not going to be that bad.* We all listened intensely as they repeated back the oath to the captain.

Of course, that is part of the program, as well. As soon as the captain finished giving them the oath, he stated, "Drill Instructors, take your platoon!" the DIs stood there, not moving a muscle or making a sound. Their eyes were piercing and fixed straight ahead, staring through the back wall of the room. It was very eerie as the captain made his way out the door, or hatch, in Marine Corps terms. Slowly, the door started to close; it creaked as the room filled with fear and anxiety. The door finally slammed shut, 'Bang!' Right then, we had three psychotic DIs running through all of us sitting on the floor, screaming at the top of their lungs.

"Get on line!"

Complete and utter chaos ensued as we all scrambled to our feet. I'd never felt so afraid in my entire life, and that is exactly what they were trying to accomplish.

"Get on line, get on line!" kept spewing from their mouths.

Hell, nobody knew what they were talking about. We finally started to get the point after spotting the parallel lines drawn in front of the racks. Scrambling to the 'line' each recruit stared across at another seeing the absolute fear in the eyes of the recruits across from me, it was apparent we were all terrified. It has to be one of the most stressful situations human beings allow themselves to be in, never mind volunteer for.

"Dump your gear!"

The DIs made us pour everything out of our bags onto the floor. All of the items, near 50 or so, scattered everywhere and mixed with the guys to our sides, adding to the confusion. Instantly, they started sounding off on each item, one by one, that we should have in our possession. They used military terms and none of us knew what the fuck they were talking about. None of us knew what an e-tool, or any of the other gear in the duffle bag was called. As you were scrambling to find your shower shoes, one of these DIs would be screaming at you.

"Where are your shower shoes, recruit?"

They stayed on you, asking why it took you so long to hold up and show your shower shoes or e-tool. When they were really pissed, they would put their 'smoky,' a.k.a. hat, directly underneath your nose and keep it there as they yelled at the top of their lungs like you had wronged them in another life. You felt the heat of their breath hitting your face like a wave as the moisture from their spit sprayed over your face. All the while you would be trying to figure out why these guys were so pissed off at you. All you can say is, "Yes, sir!" or, "No, sir!" It was truly a terrifying experience because your brain couldn't react or figure out what the hell was going on.

Everything was done by the numbers. It was amazing. They would dress you by saying you had five seconds to put your socks on, and then start counting down, "Five, four, three, two, one, you're done!" I heard this statement a million times during my three-month stay at boot camp.

The DIs scared you so badly sometimes that you just couldn't think rationally. We were given very specific instructions on how to shave. "You will begin shaving from the top of your ear, all the way over!" There were no such things as sideburns. As we ran into the head (the bathroom), one guy took the instructions so literally that he shaved from the top of his ears all the way over and shaved off his eyebrows. He seriously shaved off his eyebrows because he heard them say start from the top of your ear and shave across. This is exactly the kind of fear they inflicted. The DIs swarmed him like killer bees.

"What the hell did you do to yourself, recruit?"

"Are you wanting us to send you home?"

That recruit was berated and made an example of for the next three days. I have to admit, he did look pretty hilarious having no eyebrows.

The rest of the platoon was on line with the DIs right in our faces, uncomfortably close, shining flashlights on our faces looking for a hint of stubble. Ninety-nine percent of the platoon was sent back to the head to re-shave. At that time, I had a baby face and had never needed to shave before. The DI inspecting me got pissed that he couldn't find a hair on me. "You're fine, recruit," was all he could murmur with aggravation in his voice.

As recruits, we were required to do things a certain way. My platoon had to carry two canteens with us at all times and be ready to drink on command. We drank, pissed, shit, shaved, ate, and slept on command. Individual control was relinquished, as the Marine Corps and these sadistic, badass drill instructors now owned us.

The first time we filled our canteens, the drill instructors barked out, "Fill up your canteens! Do it now!" so we scrambled to the head to fill them up. All faucets flowed as we tried to finish as quickly as possible. All of us were done within 20 seconds, but still got an earful. Like bumper cars we knocked into each other throughout boot camp, and this time was no different. Each of us hustled to get back on line. The DI barked out the next command.

"Drink now! Do it!"

Everyone tipped their canteen back and started chugging water like they had been in the desert all day. We tried to get the water down as fast as possible. Everyone tipped their canteen back to drink except one recruit. This really stood out since he had not made the same movement as everyone else. Of course, the DIs saw that he wasn't drinking and converged on him. He had a look of total confusion and horror as he saw the rest of us drinking from our canteens.

"What are you doing, recruit?"

They swarmed in on him like bees; he had all three of these hard asses all over him. Stoically, he stood there and didn't move a muscle. The rest of us had finished our first canteen and watched the ensuing craziness. He had misunderstood the command to "Fill them up now. Do it!" Unfortunately for this mistaken recruit, he thought they wanted him to fill up his canteens with urine, not water, so he had pissed in and filled them up. The stress put on us was immense and intense. I thought they were going to crucify this poor guy. He was an absolute monster, too, a pitch black recruit, heavily muscled and standing about 6'3". He was no one you would want to mess with, but was almost brought to his knees with the stress the hard asses put on him. They verbally assaulted him for what felt like an hour before finally administering the physical punishment of the quarterdeck.

A number of recruits projectile vomited, unused to drinking so much water at once. At least seven or eight recruits launched while standing there on line trying to force down all of the water these drill instructors made us drink. It was a close one for me as well. My stomach felt swollen like one of those starving kids from an Africa charity commercial. I knew that I couldn't take one more drop of water or I'd puke myself. I felt bad for the guys getting sick. We knew from now on that they could, and would, force us to drink this amount of water on a constant basis throughout boot camp.

When you fuck up in boot camp, nine times out of ten, you end up on the quarterdeck. The quarterdeck was situated at the top of the squad bay, right next to the on-duty DIs' sleeping quarters. It had a door and a red hand painted on a square wooden board with specific instructions on how to go about getting the DI when they were in their quarters. The instructions consisted of slapping your hand on the red hand three times and then barking out, "Good morning, sir. Recruit Milano requests permission to speak with the drill instructor, sir."

The rest of the squad bay was bunk bed racks that were perfectly aligned with 20 or so bunks on each side. Most times we were punished individually on the quarterdeck. The rest of the time we were punished as a platoon. Even if one person fucked up, the rest of the platoon usually paid for it. This was to instill the knowledge that you are only as strong as your weakest link and that if one person fucks up, the entire platoon could end up dead in a combat situation.

My platoon consisted of around sixty-five recruits. On the quarterdeck, they gave commands at random and just wore you out.

"Leg lifts, do it!"

"Mountain climbers, do it now!"

"Push-ups!"

"Jumping jacks!"

"Leg lifts!"

We flailed around on the quarterdeck looking like complete imbeciles. Every time we went up there we became so exhausted and drenched with sweat that we could hardly stand. I spent many hours on that damn quarterdeck. My usual transgression was that my weapon was not clean enough.

Each member of the platoon was required to write home and tell their families that they were fine and not being mistreated, which I thought was pretty funny. They even had a template letter to copy verbatim. I'm sure we all wondered, "What was mistreatment?" We had reached Parris Island and were safe and healthy.

It was just my luck that we received a lecture from the senior drill instructor, Staff Sggt Funk, telling us to inform all family members not to send any care packages. They wanted to control our diets and it would be highly frowned upon to receive anything. They are not allowed to keep a care package from you, but after that speech, no one wanted any part of getting one.

Not one fucking hour later, a package arrived for me that was, lo and behold, from the Beast. A friggin' care package filled with all the shit the DIs did not want you to eat. I dared not take one bite, not one sniff of the things inside that box. Talk about something coming at the exact wrong time. Way to go, Betty! Her reach of causing me anguish knew no limits. It was a perfect example of how wrong our relationship had been from the very start. If anyone ever believed in karma or 'signs,' getting a care package from the person you can't stand on the same day you are told not to have anyone send you one speaks volumes.

Our mornings started the same way each and every day. At 4:30 a.m., the lights came on as the DIs banged on trash cans, making their way down the squad bay, barking out, "Get on line, get on line, get on line!" We would literally jump out of the rack from a dead sleep onto the floor and scramble to the line in front of the racks. Most of us were 18-21 years old. Everyone would stand there sporting morning wood. Each and every one of us had raging hard-ons from all of the physical activity and lack of sex or masturbation. The worst part is that you couldn't do anything about it. It's not like you could push it down with your hands trying to make it relax. Without a moment to think, you flew out of your bunk and in no time you were standing there at attention on line. It was absolutely hilarious as 65 guys stood there at full attention, and I mean *full* attention. We would have made a great erectile dysfunction commercial.

Go down; go down, I would say in my head to no avail.

Within a minute or so of the DIs yelling at you, it would finally go soft.

They would commence the daily routine of dressing you by the numbers.

"Get your socks on now, do it!"

"Five, four, three, two, one, you're done!"

Each item of clothing was put on the same way. They yelled at us to form up outside, four deep and twelve wide, in perfect alignment. "Right face, forward march!" Each one of us marched in unison, more synchronized each day. The first thing on the agenda was to go to chow. Meals were always interesting as you were only given a very short amount of time to eat. It was a matter of a few minutes and you needed every bit of food you could put into your body because you burned off so many calories during the day. Each day, at every meal, they yelled, "You're done, you're done! Get outside now, do it!" The last guy in line always got screwed because he got maybe one minute to eat.

Each day we marched back to the barracks. You could hear each heel from the platoon hit exactly at the same time, one click. They would take us back to get dressed for Physical Training (PT). It was the same routine; we started each day with the daily seven: jumping jacks, push-ups, mountain climbers, trunk twisters, alternating toe touches, flutter kicks, and the dreaded leg lifts. Then the DIs would take us out for a three-mile run while calling out the cadence.

"Momma and Papa were lying in bed, Momma rolled over and this is what she said: give me some PT; it's good for you, it's good for me."

These chants became more and more creative and vulgar each week. Drilling and marching made up a great deal of our day. After a while, your body can get used to anything and this all became routine.

One of the DIs' favorite torture treatments, when a recruit messed up, was to make all of us bring our mattresses downstairs and outside. None of the mattresses were allowed to hit the deck in any way or we had to run back upstairs to the squad bay and do it all over again. This was so hard; we could barely get our arms around the mattresses and they were pretty heavy. Up and down the stairs we ran as they saw recruits letting their mattress hit the deck. In order to keep mine off the deck, as my arms started to quiver from holding on to it for so long, I bit into the mattress and held it up with my teeth. Nobody wanted to be the recruit who made everyone keep doing this torturous exercise.

The DIs became very creative as we got into better and better condition. From making us take our mattresses downstairs to having us outside flipping around in the sand pits, pretending to be crabs as we did flutter kicks and mountain climbers, they stepped up their game as we progressed.

Toward the end of boot camp, things actually became comical. We became desensitized to the Dis. They could make us pay on the quarterdeck, but we were in such phenomenal condition that they could no longer exhaust us.

In one instance, I hadn't cleaned my weapon well enough, as usual. Fully expecting to go to the quarterdeck, I was a bit surprised when Drill Instructor Webb ordered me to the big gear locker. This locker was situated behind the quarterdeck and was one of the few places that had a door. Sgt Webb was a true, hard-ass DI and met me in there to teach me a lesson.

"Boy, I'm so tired of checking your weapon and finding it dirty, I want you to remember to clean it."

He reared back and his fist cut through the air, landing squarely in my solar plexus. The sound 'thud' came from my body but unfortunately did not have the effect he was looking for. Coming into boot camp at 186 pounds, I'd been chiseled down to a lean 140 pounds with not one ounce of fat on me. This probably would have hurt at any other time in my life, but the same DI had just made me do thousands of leg lifts over the past two months. My stomach was like iron; I didn't even budge. This, of course, pissed him off to no end.

He reared back and hit me again, so I pretended to gasp and lean forward, but he knew it didn't faze me at all.

"Come with me, Milano!"

I was in big trouble and the next thing I knew, I was over a commode doing inverted handstand presses. Each time I had to dip my head in the cool commode water.

"Get that head all the way in, Whirly Bird," he barked.

You know, the bird thing people have on their desks where the bird dips its beak in the water comes back up and dunks back to the water. It felt like I had done maybe 25 or so inverted presses into the commode before he finally yelled at me to get to my feet. These DIs were a little warped, tasked with creating physical killing machines.

During the entire time at boot camp, Rob stood directly across from me each day in the squad bay. He watched me shrink to an absolutely hard, ripped Marine who could run sub-six-minute miles. I was physically at the peak of conditioning. Rob would tell me later that he saw me change every day, actually saw my muscles come out more and more each day we were there.

One of our recruits happened to get into more trouble than the rest of us. His name was Parker and he was a tiny guy whose dream in life was to be a Marine. He had been in ROTC all through high school, but that really didn't help him too much in boot camp. At the head of your rack was a footlocker that held every item you owned. The footlocker was to be secured at all times, never unlocked, and Parker left his unsecured a number of times.

Sgt Rios decided to make him pay for this screw up by making him hold the footlocker out in front of his body with just his arms. Parker started to shake almost uncontrollably trying to hold it up.

"Keep it up, Parker!"

He was going to make Parker suffer and never forget to lock it again. After a while, his arms gave out and the footlocker hit his legs. It didn't stop Sgt Rios from having him do it again and again. This went on for 30 or so. I felt bad for Parker, but that guy had fucked up for so long during boot camp, he almost got a blanket party.

A blanket party is done to a recruit who keeps screwing up repeatedly. Usually, the rest of the platoon is punished for the fuck-ups, so in order to get the message across, a blanket party is sometimes the answer. At a pre-determined time, four guys from the platoon would slowly sneak up on the rack of the guilty party. At the same time, each one grabbed the corners of the blanket and pulled down tight to hold the recruit in his rack, pinned down. The rest of the platoon would line up and take turns throwing punches to the blanket, never the face. This usually got the message across and straightened the recruit out, more so than the usual discipline from the DIs. Whenever possible, Marine Corp problems are solved internally.

Chapter 9

Each Marine needs to become qualified with an M-16, and it was our time to head out to the rifle range. We had very detailed classroom instruction as well as one-on-one training on the proper technique for becoming a lethal weapon with your rifle. I'd never fired a rifle before boot camp, so I didn't have 'bad habits.' They want you to be good at killing. One of the most critical parts of shooting with efficiency is to control your breathing and never know when the bullet will fire out of your weapon. "Squeeze, don't pull your trigger," was repeated to us over and over at the firing range. I scored in the expert category, which is the highest mark. Under that is sharpshooter and then marksman. We shot from 200, 300, and 500 yards.

After we qualified, we were sent down range to put the targets in for the next batch of recruits to shoot. We were all behind a large embankment that protected us from the bullets coming down range. The targets were on a 3x5-foot matting. The target holders were really heavy, and it took some effort to get them up in the air. One of the DIs yelled, "Milano!" Never really knowing what the hell they wanted, I immediately ran up to him.

"Recruit Milano reporting as ordered, sir!"

I had failed to see where I was standing. The metal cage came down and hit me right on the side of the neck and shoulder blade. I was fine for a second, but then everything went dark.

Waking up on the ground, they had dragged me to a puddle and put me in the water. They called the ambulance, as I had been knocked out for a few minutes.

Embarrassed by the whole ordeal, I asked to not be taken to the hospital, but the DI ordered me to get in the ambulance and get examined. With all of the fights I had been in growing up, this was the first time I'd been knocked out completely. After being checked out thoroughly by the medical staff, I returned to my platoon.

There was one other instance in which I needed medical assistance during my stay in boot camp. One night I woke up with my cheek very swollen. Reaching up to check it out, it felt like a golf ball had been shoved into my face. It was hard as a rock. Knowing it had to be something pretty significant, I got up and let the fire watch recruit know I needed to wake up the duty DI. Toward the end of boot camp, we had a fire watch, someone walking around the squad bay while the rest of us slept. We all took turns with shifts lasting one hour each night.

Making my way toward the quarterdeck, I felt very nervous waking up the DI, but knew it had to be done. Smacking my hand against the red hand on the wall, and with a quieter than usual voice, woke up the DI. He took a quick look at my face and ordered an ambulance to pick me up and take me to the hospital immediately. The doctor told me a spider had bitten me and that he was going to have to drain it. Lying back on the bed as he took out an absolutely massive needle, I could see it coming closer and closer to my face as I prepared for the pain. The golf ball-sized bite was really close to my eye, so I could see the needle enter my face.

As it slowly made its way into the mass, I heard a 'pop' as the doctor slid the needle deep into the bite lesion. Surprisingly, I didn't even feel the needle going into my wound. The doctor pulled the needle plunger back and I watched the poisonous puss filling up the hub of the needle. It was really disgusting hearing it go out of my face like that. Instantly I felt relief as he removed the pressure that had been making my cheek tight from the bite. They let me return to the squad bay right away and the swelling was almost gone by the time they called Reveille.

One particular day was a bit different from the others. We learned that we were going into the gas chamber that day. A number of recruits were anxious about what was ahead of us. Not knowing what the gas chamber would be like, I wasn't particularly nervous. We marched out and received a demonstration on how to don our gas masks. The process seemed easy enough; we slid on the rubber masks fitted with two filters to keep all the chemical agents from reaching our lungs. Some of the nasty toxins that had been developed by the Russians were no joke. Nerve gas was the really scary one, so it was critical that we know how to use these gas masks.

After receiving instruction on how to put our masks on, blow poisons out of them and drink water with them on, we readied ourselves to enter the chamber. We entered the building and saw haze in the air, but breathed normally with our masks. The platoon stood looking at each other, anticipating what would happen next. Any exposed skin started to burn like a terrible sunburn. It grew worse and worse the longer we were in the chamber. The dreaded, "Remove your masks!" order came from the instructor.

Fuck! Is all I could think at the time. There was no way to hold your breath as they made you sound off next. Taking in a massive amount of air filled with CS gas, a.k.a. tear gas, my lungs, eyes, and nose started to burn. It felt like I was drowning in air and couldn't catch my breath. It was very similar to the feeling of holding your breath too long while under water. Panic started to kick in for some of the recruits and they began pushing toward the doorway. The instructor yelled out, "Stop panicking! Remain calm and you will get through this!" Some of the guys started to lose it. The door finally opened and we made our way outside. A number of recruits started vomiting immediately. Snot rolled out of my nostrils like never before. It stretched all the way down to the ground. My eyes watered and my skin felt like it was on fire.

We all eventually recovered and felt normal again after a few hours. The purpose of the exercise was to prove beyond a shadow of a doubt that these gas masks worked and were critical to your survival in a chemical warfare situation. I wondered how awful our world would have to become if we had to wear these gas masks and fight our enemies. I envisioned an apocalyptic world in which no one was left except the people in gas masks trying to kill each other. This thought resonated with me for the entirety of my time in the Marine Corps.

One of the final exercises we did as recruits was to go out into the field and practice basic military tactics to get ready to join the Marine Corps fleet and be a weapon for the U.S. We learned how to stagger our positions and why that was important when going out on a tactical mission. We also learned how to put our tents up and how to eat MREs (meals ready to eat). The DIs gave us less than sixty seconds to eat our whole meal the entire seven days we were out training in the field. This was also our first taste of 'humping' which was hiking at a high rate of speed carrying all of our gear. Even in the shape we were in from boot camp, humping for 20 miles really tested our resolve. It's much more of a mental challenge than a physical one.

Our platoon learned some pretty effective hand-to-hand combat moves out in the field. We had a fourth-degree black belt in Jiu Jitsu, who had trained in Okinawa, taking us through numerous scenarios as we took each other on to practice what we had learned. Having fought so much as a kid, I thought I knew how to fight, but the moves this guy taught us blew my mind. We have so many weak points as humans that we don't consider when facing off against our enemy. We learned how to hurt and kill someone as quickly as possible. It was a rush learning how to kill so effectively with your bare hands.

The worst thing that can happen in combat is to be without your weapon. It's possible to occasionally run out of ammunition. The next thing we learned was how to utilize our rifle in close combat to bash our enemy's head in if needed. We went through a number of moves and 'effective kill' scenarios. At the end of the day, we went into a ring and utilized padded poles called pugil sticks against each other to practice what we had learned. We were given football helmets and gloves to protect ourselves from getting really injured. I had noticed the recruits all doing the same thing each time they squared off against each other during practice. Each time they gave it their all as soon as the whistle sounded. Like clockwork, each recruit swung downward with the most forward end of the stick and usually hit each other at the same time.

It was surprising to see everyone doing exactly the same thing. I'd already decided what I was going to do when stepping into the ring. Finally, it was my turn and I stood across from a recruit named Jones. Waiting with a tight grip on my pugil stick, the DI blew the whistle. Immediately, I jumped fast to the left, knowing that Jones was going to swing directly at my head. He missed badly and left himself vulnerable, wide open for a counter hit. Coming down with my left side, I struck him in the temple area and he dropped to the ground immediately. I went undefeated that day using the same technique against my fellow recruits. For some reason, things slowed down for me in that ring and I felt comfortable there, as opposed to the usual stress of boot camp. It felt awesome to knock the shit out of my fellow recruits and dominate them that day.

At the end of the day, we packed up our gear and made the 15 mile hump back to the barracks. We finished the hump and our time in the field at boot camp came to an end. Platoon 1066 would have a hot meal at the chow hall and we were super psyched about it.

Finally, after three long months of running endlessly, pushing our bodies to the limit physically and mentally, the day arrived when Platoon 1066 graduated and became full-fledged Marines. We had worn out the heels on our boots from 13 weeks of marching every day. The final week of boot camp consisted of shining our boots and brass items as much as possible and marching. We felt the excitement in the squad bay that last week. All of us knew how hard it was to go through what we had been through together. For most in the squad bay, it was the hardest thing we would ever have to experience in our young lives. Nothing had ever tested me like that and it showed me that I was made of much more than I had realized.

It was absolutely exhilarating to finally be at the end of the hardest challenge I had ever undertaken. There is nothing like the feeling of walking across the parade deck at Parris Island and becoming a United States Marine; it's like walking on air. The morning of graduation we put on our dress uniforms and marched in front of everyone who attended that day. The DIs were actually nice to us that morning and we didnt know how to react. One helped me get squared away with my uniform. We had a few recruits who couldn't cut it and dropped out during training. Marine Corps boot camp is not cut out for everyone who attempts it.

With boot camp in the rearview, I was ready to start my life now. Being 18 years old, I'd been given every reason to believe the future was bright and that I could accomplish anything I put my mind to, with few exceptions. The excitement and pride that ran through my veins made me feel as if I could conquer the world. Rob and I said we would catch up with each other back in Lawrenceburg, as we wanted to visit our friends.

Just before graduation, I received a letter from Betty telling me she would be there for the ceremony. At the time I thought it was nice and didn't really think too much about it. She drove down with her mother and Melissa. They came a few days early and spent time on Hilton Head Island, a vacation place pretty close to Parris Island.

None of them recognized me as I had lost more than 40 pounds during those three months. I had seven days off right after boot camp before needing to report and start Infantry Training School (ITS). Betty and I drove together followed by Melissa and Nicole. We had traveled at least for a while when I looked back for Melissa's car, which was nowhere to be found. We decided to circle around to try and find them, to no avail. Since it was dark, and I was emotionally spent from graduating, we decided to get a hotel room and rest.

During boot camp, the drill instructors were all over us from 4:30 a.m. until we fell asleep at night. You thought about masturbating all the time to relieve the sexual stress you were under but wouldn't dare do it because you were surrounded by 60 other guys. I could only imagine the horror you would feel if a DI caught you jerking off.

Needless to say, I was so ready to have some sex! Being 18, at the peak of physical condition, with no sexual release for the past three months, I was about to explode. As much as I wasn't attracted to Betty, I could have had sex with a tree trunk at that moment. She was all too ready, too. We were just about to get undressed when I looked her straight in the face and asked the all-important and critical question.

"Are you still on the pill? Do I need to go get condoms?"

I was ready to go to the store and get condoms or whatever we needed to have sex. She looked me straight in the eyes and said, "Yes, I've been on the pill the whole time you've been away." This became the biggest lie ever told to me in my young adult life. What I hadn't known is that she had planned this out to perfection; she knew deep down that she had no chance of us being together and threw a Hail Mary. There was no reason to think she was lying, as she had been on birth control for quite a while. I'd made it very clear that I had no intentions of becoming a father or getting married until I had a college degree and had myself established in a career. The last thing in the world I wanted was to be a father at 18.

Betty was incredibly intelligent and obviously knew this would be the last week we would be together.

The Marine Corps sends you off to foreign countries to defend the United States' interests and be a global peacekeeper. In other words, I would soon be gone and unavailable to her. She knew this was her one chance to have a tie with me, to get her hooks in, per se. The Beast set her twisted trap.

I fucked Betty and it was over within minutes. We had

sex a number of times that night and each time I emptied inside of her. The Beast and I got on the road first thing in the morning and headed to Lawrenceburg. It was a wonderful week of seeing friends from high school. I looked and felt great and had every reason in the world to feel positive toward life. Unfortunately, during this week we also had unprotected sex over and over again.

The last day of my leave, I tried to get Betty ready for the fact that she and I wouldn't see each other for a long time. In my mind, never again. I didn't want to be a total dick, either. I explained that I would have to do Infantry Training School and that most Marines spend a great deal of time on tours overseas, so there was no telling when we would see each other again. All of this was true, leaving me with a clean conscience as I headed back.

After my leave was up I reported for duty at Camp Geiger and started Infantry Training School. Everything felt so positive and happy. I was finally in control of my life and ready to start my military career. ITS was just barely a step up from boot camp.

Chapter 10

ITS is where you learn to use most of the weapons the Marine Corps has in its arsenal. Each and every day you fire thousands of rounds of ammunition. At ITS we were assigned to a training sergeant who took us to the firing ranges and training courses. It was funny; he would yell at us each day to do shit. At first, you can't help but call him 'Sir' because it is so ingrained from boot camp, but he was enlisted just like we were. Our training platoon trained all week long and lived in old-school barracks. We weren't allowed to leave the base until the weekends, but the way I saw it, we actually had weekends off, which was awesome compared to the three months without a day

off.

This guy was hilarious to look at because it looked like he wore eyeliner all the time. Sgt Brooks was a huge, hulking type of guy who was a bit rough. He was pretty tough on us, but I wasn't sure why, exactly. After a few weeks, he started to chill out and become a normal guy.

We had long days of training, but they were pretty amazing. I trained with and got to fire all types of the most deadly and powerful weapons in the world. We were issued our basic weapon, an M16, and it was locked to our racks. ITS is where you learn how to fight and kill like a Marine. We fired our M16s, 50 caliber machine guns, and a Mark 19, which is an automatic grenade launcher. You can feel the power when you fire these formidable weapons. The destruction they cause when hitting targets downrange…it's hard to fathom what they would do to a human being on the other end. It was surreal, the amount of ammo we went through while training. Each day started with a hump of 10- 20 miles out to the specialized target ranges. Our ammunition would be piled up waiting for us. Thousands upon thousands of rounds were at our disposal...our tax dollars hard at work.

One day we were out at the range and one of my Marine colleagues started talking crazy. He mentioned wanting to see blood and feeling the need to turn around and start lighting up some of his fellow Marines waiting their turn to shoot. This was a New York kid, and it was hard to tell if he was serious, but he had thousands of rounds of ammo at his fingertips. A few more things came out of his mouth that finally concerned us enough that my buddy, Cohen, and I jumped on top of him.

He struggled and tried to get out of our grip, but by then a few more Marines had come to help hold him down. It was chaos on a range of weapons and almost countless amounts of ammo; the sergeant of the range came running. In the heat of the moment it was hard to describe to the sergeant what exactly was going on, but it finally sunk in why we were restraining him. We held our fellow Marine down until we were able to secure him with some belts. They called for the MPs to come and get him. It finally hit me the amount of damage and lives he could have taken that day had he turned on us, and that they didn't screen people for mental disorders before joining the Marine Corps. It was hard to believe he made it through boot camp.

While at ITS, I developed a routine. A bunch of my buddies, including Rob, would head out to town and rent a cottage on the beach twenty miles from the base and drink like rock stars on weekend leave. We had an absolute blast each weekend. It was the kind of freedom I had only dreamed of. The camaraderie with my guys was amazing. We were able to get closer than we could at boot camp because we were actually allowed to talk and get to know each other.

It was so obvious that we were brand new Marines. Our haircuts were ridiculously high and tight and we walked around not knowing where to go or what to do. I found the beach house that we rented one weekend and it became our home away from home on weekends. There was a core group of eight to ten of us who went to the beach cottage. We had a great time at that house. We partied night and day, swam in the ocean and chased girls at local bars. Things were pretty good as I became accustomed to military life.

One night, I got the one phone call from Betty that I never wanted to get while at the barracks. It felt weird; I didn't expect to hear from her anymore.

"Mark, I have to see you; it's really important and we need to speak face to face."

A pit grew in my stomach and a sick feeling came over me; I didn't want to see her at all. As much as possible, I tried to put her off because I was having way too much fun, and as far as I was concerned, things were over between us. I thought it was bullshit, but agreed to let her come see me the following weekend. My buddies and I did our normal weekend thing, renting our beach house, and I gave her directions to the cottage.

A car slowly pulled up and a sense of dread took over my entire body. I was not happy at all to see her. We went for a walk on the beach and I was determined that no matter what, I would not sleep with her anymore. It was over. Then, out of her mouth came, "Mark, I'm pregnant."

Holy fucking shit. I couldn't believe it. I felt like a train had run over me. What do you say to that?

"You're fucking kidding me, right," I blurted out? "You said you were on the pill!"

She went into this long, drawn-out speech, rambling over and over about the birth control pill not being completely effective and that we happened to be the one percent for which it was ineffective.

Fucking bullshit, I knew she was lying. I couldn't believe she had done this to me. Knowing that it was over, she purposely got pregnant so that she could trap me. She had looked me right in the eye and lied to my face that night in the hotel, the day of graduation. I felt devastated at the fate that had befallen me. My fucking dick put me in the worst spot possible; how could I have let this happen?

Immediately, I went into 'we have to do something about this' mode. At 18, I was not ready, nor did I want to have a child with someone I couldn't stand in the first place. I pleaded with her to get an abortion. Desperate to have a chance at achieving my goals and dreams, I begged and pleaded with her. Knowing full well that this would affect me for the rest of my life, panic set in and my pleas fell on deaf ears. The Beast didn't budge, didn't even contemplate the idea of it. Of course not, she had planned it all along. Checkmate, she had me and had leverage. The real games began at that moment. She went back to Kentucky and my mind raced every second of the day. What the hell was I going to do?

Systematically, the Beast started pressuring me about getting married. She ramped up a bit more each and every week. Married? A sickness came over me like nothing I had ever felt. The words coming out of her lips caused me a mini heart attack each time she said them. My heart palpitated when she spoke; I would lose my breath and have a hard time talking. Her excuse was that she wanted me to marry her or her family name would be tarnished in the small town of Lawrenceburg.

Her uncle had a big real estate company and was tied into the county government. Each week passed by feeling like another cinder block was added to my back. Full-court press at all times, she was unrelenting in her approach. Each conversation was tweaked to add more and more pressure. It was absolutely unbearable; someone with that kind of resolve could not be held back forever. She put all her chips on the table, went all in, and would bend me to her will if it killed me. Guilt was her weapon of choice. She couldn't be pregnant and not married. My god that would be the end of the fucking world!

We got closer and closer to graduation, but the cottage just wasn't as fun and life didn't seem so bright anymore. Betty had taken a bit of light out of my life and it felt like a cloud was over me. Instead of enjoying my life, I grew to dread it.

We continued our training regime and ramped up to more intense military exercises. Sgt Brooks kept getting me and a guy named Tyler confused. Tyler constantly got in trouble and when Sgt Brooks yelled out, "Milano! What the fuck are you doing?" Tyler never corrected him. It was always me who had to speak up and correct him, saying, "That's not Milano, I'm Milano!" After a while, Tyler and I became friends because Sgt Brooks confused us every day the entire time we were in ITS.

Tyler's family lived in Myrtle Beach, South Carolina, and one weekend he invited me home to come hang out at their home. Myrtle Beach was just over 120 miles from the base. We discovered that Tyler's military ID card actually looked more like me than it did him. The beautiful thing was that he was 22 years old. A light bulb went off over our heads. He gave me his ID and got a replacement, and I used it for the next three years until I turned 21. Studying his info until I knew every number on his ID, I had his date of birth, Social Security number and everything down pat. During the three years I used that ID, not once did anyone ever challenge it; it was amazing.

From that moment on, I could get into any bar and buy any kind of alcohol from any store I wanted. It was amazing that his ID looked just like me. Tyler and I went to Myrtle Beach a few times when the cottage wasn't available to rent. It was fun to party at the beach and be away from base, not be around all the other Marines. Tyler's younger sister took quite a liking to me. She must have been around 15 or so. As we were hanging out watching TV, she reached over one time and started grabbing at my Johnson. I couldn't believe it, but I also didn't stop her. She wanted me to fuck her, but I wasn't going down that path. The thought of touching any girl sexually since the Beast had dropped the hammer really scared me, never mind that I was only 18.

The day finally arrived and we graduated from ITS. After making it through boot camp and graduating ITS together, Rob was being shipped out to Guantanamo Bay, Cuba, to start his duty station. We wouldn't see each other again until we got out of the Marine Corps. It was time for me to join my regular unit, 1st Battalion, 2nd Marines, B Company.

My ride was in a cattle car, which was basically an 18-wheeler truck with a trailer built just for hauling Marines. It had a number of bars to hold onto and not many seats.

They dropped me off at the admin building for 1st Battalion, 2nd Marines. The admin people processed me and told me to go to the barracks with my gear. My buddy, Tyler, got assigned to 3rd Battalion, 6th Marines. We continued to stay in touch and go on weekend trips to Myrtle Beach for a few years.

After checking in with the platoon sergeant, he told me what room I was assigned to and I began my career as a fleet Marine. I was so lucky to have the privilege of sharing a room with Cornelius Frank and Trevor Glenn. Both were dark green Marines (black guys). Glenn was at least 6'2" and Frank was a thick, muscular guy who I eventually found out wouldn't hurt a fly...unless you messed with one of his buddies.

As I slowly opened the door and walked in, I saw that the rooms were set up for three men. All of the curtains were drawn tight; it was dark and very quiet and the smell of gin emanated throughout the room. As I made my way through, I noticed bottle after bottle of Tanqueray lying about everywhere. Neither Frank nor Glenn were moving a muscle. They were both tanked out of their minds. Not wanting to wake them up or disturb them on our first meeting, I wasn't sure what to do. Setting my gear down, I made my way outside. After a while, I went back into the room. Frank woke up and said hello, and he was definitely feeling rough.

"Hey, I'm your new roommate," I said. From that moment on, he never called me anything besides 'roommate.' I actually loved that and knew it was going to be a good match. Luckily, it was Friday and my platoon was assigned to cut loose on liberty for the weekend. It was great to have a weekend off after finishing infantry school.

This set a precedent for how things would go, living with my roommates. When I finally met and talked with them, we hit it off immediately. We all bonded right from the go. Glenn was a huge Anita Baker fan. He sat and listened to her for hours. Whenever he had a few too many drinks, he sang along with Anita and yelled out, "I love you Anita Baker!" It was too funny. Frank and I also became fast friends. He looked out for me whenever we went out and partied; he treated me like a brother. He always had my back and I really looked up to him. Frank had tattoos on both arms. One was a Marine Corps bulldog and the other was of the Grim Reaper. You could barely see the tattoos because Frank was black, but he loved them. He was from Baltimore, Maryland, and became one of the most beloved members of our platoon.

We spent a great deal of time partying and drinking it up whenever possible. There were many mornings when we had to go to physical training and would take quick breaks to projectile vomit before returning to running formation and continuing our runs. The platoon went on many humps. It was really one of the most dreaded things to do in the military, carrying a pack on your back with your weapon and walking very quickly for 20 to 30 miles at a time. Frank and Glenn would rap the Beastie Boys' *License to Ill* album verbatim. I was amazed that they knew all of the words as if they had written the songs themselves.

These humps really tested our endurance and stamina because we had a helmet, heavy pack, weapon and boots weighing us down. It was a mental challenge because we never knew exactly how far we were going, that is the idea. In a hostile environment, you may have to walk out to save your life. The pack felt like someone pulling down on our shoulder blades constantly. Our feet ached and throbbed. "Stretch it out," we heard when we went on these humps. Even though we were 'walking' per se, we were actually going as fast as someone doing a slow jog. Depending on the mood of the company commander, we could expect 20 percent of the company to not finish the entire hump. People fell over from heat exhaustion all the time. Some of my fellow Marines' eyes rolled back in their heads. Sometimes a hard-ass sergeant would come yell at the poor guy who fell out of the hump. It was sad. Some guy was just lying on the side of the road thinking he was going to die and somebody is yelling in his ear, "Get up, you fucking pussy!"

Out in the field, I hung around Frank, Dave, Glenn, Todd, and Tony. Being 'out in the field' is what most civilians think Marines do all the time. We go out in the woods and play G.I. Joe. We shoot shit up on different ranges and practice killing the enemy. One of the common things we participated in while out in the field was a 'skull drag.' Each platoon sent in a number of Marines to square off against another platoon in a pit of some sort. The last man standing won. Frank was absolutely awesome at this. He could take on three other Marines at the same time. Our platoon usually won these games as we had some badass guys.

The events were extremely brutal though and people got hurt all the time. One skull drag I remember very vividly. We were going up against Weapons Platoon. These guys were monsters as they usually pick big guys to be in Weapons Platoon. They carry all of the M60s and mortars so they want guys who can handle the weight. There was one guy named Schofield who was just absolutely horrific. He was a great guy, but it came down to him and Frank squaring off. They battled for a long time before Frank finally got the better of him. Dave started calling Frank "Frankbo" from that moment on.

Glenn twisted up his knee while we were out in the field and the next thing we knew he received a medical discharge and was out of the Marine Corps. It shocked Frank and me as we had a great roommate situation and all of a sudden, he was gone. No more singing from Glenn, no more partying with our roommate. We were sad to see him leave, but that is a way of life in the Marine Corps. You sign up for a four-year enlistment, so people were coming and going all of the time.

Each Thursday we had room inspection at the barracks. Frank and I had a great system; we took each part of the room and made it look flawless in no time. I took the bathroom and sink area, making sure to shine any metal parts. That was the key to making a place look especially clean. We had a secret weapon as we utilized Mop & Glo on the floor. No one else bothered to buy a non-issued cleaner like we did, but our room sparkled. Frank was meticulous when it came to his clothes. His uniforms always looked great and were ironed or dry cleaned, hanging in the closet perfectly. I adopted his same approach and my uniforms always looked great. He went as far as to iron his civilian clothes; his jeans had a perfect crease whenever we went out to party.

Normally each week Frank and I cleaned our room faster than everyone else in the platoon. The gunnery sergeant, a.k.a. "gunny," usually conducted the inspections. Most times we had a pretty cool gunny who took a quick look at our room and commented on what a great job we had done. Unfortunately, a new gunny sergeant took over the company. He wanted to make his presence known to the Bravo Company, somewhat like a dog marking his territory or expressing dominance. This happened frequently in the Marine Corps as we always had new commanders and platoon sergeants rotating through.

He entered the barracks area as we lined up next to our rooms. One by one, he entered a room and found something wrong with it. You could tell he was being a dick; my fellow platoon members rolled their eyes as he made his way down toward our room. We had done an excellent job, as usual, and as he entered the room, I thought to myself that there was no way he would find something. This asshole actually carried white gloves with him.

Gunny Jones started touching everything with his white glove, hoping to find some speck of dirt or grime in order to nail us. We actually started to smile, as his attempts were futile. He caught us smiling and pulled a complete dick move. Since he couldn't find any dirt, he grabbed one of our chairs and pulled it to the center of the room. We had no idea what the hell he was doing until he reached up into the ceiling tiles, sticking his fucking finger in and pulled out dust. Frank and I looked at each other in disgust, as we knew right then and there that this guy was an asshole. He smiled as he climbed down from the chair and showed us his glove. Complete dick move. We weren't allowed to go on liberty until we passed our room inspection.

The gunny came back numerous times, failed room after room, and told us, "No one is going on liberty until all of you pass your room inspection." We threw the towel in and stopped cleaning at 2230 (10:30 p.m.). He finally quit coming over to inspect and we said fuck it. Everyone stayed at the barracks that night and didn't even bother doing any more cleaning. I was glad we didn't have any plans, not that we ever needed any to get into some kind of trouble.

Falling into a pretty comfortable routine, I knew what was in store for me in training and in cleaning our rooms and weapons. Trying to deal with Betty was a whole other story.

At my level of maturity, being 18, it was really difficult to keep her at bay. I couldn't hold out forever to the ever-increasing pressure to marry her. She was absolutely relentless in her pursuit of making me her husband. As much as I felt the brotherhood with my fellow Marines, I kept this aspect of my life secret from Frank, Dave, Todd, Miguel and the rest of the crew. I felt alone without direction from someone older telling me it was a mistake to marry someone I didn't love though she was pregnant. The day finally came when I caved to her unyielding pressure. After seven months of pregnancy, daily relentless pressure from call after call, and manipulation, I broke down and agreed to marry her. I told her I'd come to Lawrenceburg that weekend. I could feel her absolute joy and happiness through the phone and it was as completely opposite for me.

From that moment on, I carried a pit in my stomach. I knew it was a mistake and in the bottom of my soul knew I shouldn't marry someone I didn't love.

The long drive from Camp Lejeune to Lawrenceburg was one of the most painful in my life. With each mile that passed, I grew more and more anxious, trying to think of a way out of this. When I arrived in Lawrenceburg she was all smiles. Seeing her smile made me angry and nauseous. The overwhelming desire to wipe that smile off her face ran through me. I wanted to punch her straight in the face. How could she be so happy knowing how miserable she was making me? It felt like I was numb, in a fog, a very surreal experience.

After unsuccessful attempts to talk her out of it, we made our way to the courthouse. What made me agree to marry her was a simple statement. "If things don't work out and you're not happy, we can get a divorce and stay friends." She promised me, swore on our unborn child's life, that she would not be mean or freak out if things didn't work out; we would remain friends. For some reason, it seemed reasonable. I have no idea why I bought that hunk of shit statement from her, but said, "Okay." Her statement turned out to be a bigger lie than the one she had told me about being on the pill. The bullshit I swallowed would come back to haunt me later.

As we pulled up, I saw the courthouse and we got out of the car. Dreading every step, I looked down in a fog, facing a true out-of-body experience. It felt like I'd lost control of my life and my will. As the Beast and I walked up to the courthouse, I came out of it for a second and reached out touching her shoulder. I couldn't do this. No way did I want to be tied legally to this woman. She stopped and I made my final plea, "Betty, I really don't want to do this." She brushed it off like I'd said nothing.

It was shocking that a woman would marry someone who, on their wedding day says, "I don't want to do this." Nothing deterred the Beast as she reiterated that if things didn't work out, we would remain friends. It didn't calm my nerves; with every step we took, my legs became heavier. By the time we reached the top of the steps, my legs felt like they weighed a thousand pounds. My life was being stolen from me. My head tingled and I felt as if I was watching this happening to me like my own personal horror movie.

Our "wedding" was ridiculous. She didn't really know if I would go through with it, so she hadn't told anyone we were getting married. We had to find a couple of volunteers to be witnesses; it was surreal. The lips moved on the Justice of the Peace, but I couldn't hear him. Watching his lips say something I couldn't make out, I became mesmerized in a deep trance, like a mindless zombie. The Beast nudged me as the man said the vows and waited for my response. I repeated the words back. It was, by far, the unhappiest event of my entire life. Her face was beaming, she was so friggin' happy.

Two people couldn't have been at further ends of the spectrum than the Beast and I at that moment. She had won. The Justice of the Peace said, "You may kiss the bride." No chance that was going to happen, not a real kiss anyway. Reluctantly, I kissed her cheek. From that exact moment, that second, I never kissed her again, not once...not even after drinking. The thought of kissing her repulsed me. The weight of the enormous mistake I had made hit home. No one should feel that way when they get married.

The first thing I asked her was to not tell anybody we were married, hoping we could just keep it to ourselves for a while. I didn't want it to be real and was embarrassed to be married to her. If nobody knew, then it didn't really happen. How could I make it go away? She said that she wouldn't tell anyone for a while, but of course told everyone she could find, as soon as possible. She had promised, but I wasn't surprised that she had broken her first promise to me as a married couple. There was no honeymoon and I made my way out of town as quickly as possible. I was disgusted by what I'd done and knew what a mistake I had made. Immediately, I began thinking of ways to get out of it, but nothing good came to mind. I made my way back to base and tried to assess what had happened. As much as possible, I attempted to continue on with life as a single 18-year-old kid.

My buddies were absolutely shocked when I came back from Kentucky and told them I had gotten married. I'd been one of the wild, single, party guys. I hadn't disclosed my predicament to any of my Marine brothers. Now I was one of the boring, married guys that we made fun of, Marines who lived off base with their wives and kids. The term for someone who lived off base was 'brown bagger.' They had to be at the barracks by six a.m, ready for formation each day we were on duty.

Well, being mister faithful married guy didn't last too long. After the initial shock and disgust wore off, I went about life as normal. The boys and I would go out chasing the few girls around the base. Pickings were very slim. There had to be a two hundred to one ratio of guys to girls in the immediate vicinity of the base. Most girls were married to some poor Marine.

Betty lived with her parents in Kentucky, and I resided at Camp Lejeune, North Carolina. Plenty of distance existed between us, which was fine by me. She had what she wanted, a marriage license, my last name and the facade of being married. I, on the other hand, enjoyed living the single life. My buddies and I partied like absolute animals. Our metabolism and libido were off the charts from being in Marine shape, but mostly from being teenage boys. With the Beast so far away, I really didn't feel married and certainly didn't act it with any ladies who took me up on my flirting.

Chapter 11

The 1st Battalion, 2nd Marine Division was sent on a training mission to Vieques Island off of Puerto Rico for the first part of May. This was a beautiful island. It had been purchased by the U.S. government and was mostly utilized by the military for training purposes. It was largely deserted. Frank, Dave, Todd and I took our sleeping mats out after we realized that they floated. The next thing we knew we were out in the ocean off the beach area, floating on our mats. We had a great time soaking up the rays and floating out in the ocean. It was ridiculously hot and we could not get out of the sun, which became a problem for all of us later on.

Dave, Todd and I circled our new gunny on the beach. We decided that we were going to initiate him into the company by tackling him and throwing him in the ocean. The only problem was that he was one bad motherfucker. As much as we tried to get ahold of him, he tossed us around like rag dolls. Over and over we attacked him and he moved with speed and the fluidity of a ninja. We finally threw in the towel after realizing we were no match for him. The person we needed was Frank, who had found a place with some shade. Frank relaxed and chilled out under a tree while we tried to start some shenanigans.

As we walked along the beach exploring, I noticed a few coconut trees. Todd decided that he really needed to have a coconut. He jumped up onto the tree and the next thing we knew, started to shimmy up it. He had to be at least 30 feet up before he reached the coconuts. He tossed down a few and luckily didn't fall to his death, free climbing like he had. We thought it was awesome to have fresh coconuts.

It took what felt like forever to peel through the husk surrounding the fruit. We finally reached the center and got the coconut out. We tried to open it up with our knives to no avail. It was absolutely pissing us off, as we had worked so hard to get the damn things down and then out of their husks. Finally, we grabbed our helmets and started bashing the coconuts against some rocks. They finally cracked open and we yelled out, "Fuck yes!" It was like we had won the lottery. Each of us started drinking the milk and eating the meat. After all of the effort we'd put into getting to it, we all thought it sucked and were disappointed. I had no idea what we thought it would taste like. I guess we had built it up in our minds that it would be like ice cream.

We hung around the tents we had pitched earlier as the sun finally started to set when my commanding officer told the platoon sergeant to get me. I received a message from the Red Cross notifying me that my wife had given birth and that I was now the father of a little girl.

I came up with my daughter's name from watching some terrible B-movie flick with Rob while we were in high school. It had a hot, red headed chick named Jasmine. I thought she was gorgeous and never forgot her name. That was one thing Betty didn't have full control over and she actually went along with me so that is what we named her. The military doesn't allow you to just pick up and go home when a child is born while you are out on operations.

I knew it would be a few weeks before I could see Jasmine and was surprisingly very excited and happy to be a father. My buddies and I celebrated and had a beer.

They stood around and toasted me becoming a dad. As long as I didn't have to be around the mother too much, I was fine with the idea.

Betty wanted me to be there with her and decided she would do something about it. She worked her magic and the next thing I knew I was flying back to Lexington, Kentucky because my daughter was having "complications." This turned out to be greatly exaggerated, but Betty wanted me there and Betty gets what she wants. She knew how to manipulate any system. Her intelligence was above reproach and it was scary what she could accomplish if she put her mind to it. I'm not sure how she pulled this scam off on the Red Cross. She had to get a doctor to exaggerate the truth and had a way of talking people into doing things they typically wouldn't do. The next thing I knew, I was flying home to see my daughter. Arriving at the hospital, I got to see her for the first time. A rush of happiness came over me and I instantly knew, as I held her in my arms, that I loved her more than anything in my life. She had my dark skin and was a very beautiful baby. Somehow, all of her complications went away and she was almost instantly discharged from the hospital as soon as I got there.

I was ok with her lies this time because it was exciting to spend time with my daughter. My mother flew in to meet her granddaughter. She stayed in the one local hotel in Lawrenceburg and asked me to bring Jasmine there. Betty became really upset by this, and I knew my mother didn't want to be around her at all. My mother knew how I felt about Betty and it fed her animosity. She really wanted to baptize my daughter at the Catholic Church as she had found religion and wanted to impose it upon Jasmine.

I thought it was funny and didn't see what harm it

could do, but Betty threw a monumental fit when my mother suggested baptizing Jasmine. Of course, it turned into a harrowing scene as two of the most dramatic and hardheaded people were in the same room together. Needless to say, Betty won this argument and my mother returned to California.

During this time, while I was in Kentucky, Betty began talking about us living together like a real married couple. She became tired of living at home with her parents and wanted to be with her "husband." The idea of cohabitating with her sent cold chills down my spine like nails on a chalkboard. Quickly, I moved to operation Stop the Beast; I needed to do some serious dancing.

"Betty, I have a training operation coming up in the next two weeks; we can talk about living together once I return from the field."

If I hadn't had that excuse, she would have shown up at the base. Being in the military is great for evading your spouse if need be. Fortunately for me, she had no idea when I'd be training or out of the country so I could say whatever I wanted. I made her think I'd be away for the next six months to a year. It was mostly true, but the main thing it did was keep her ass in Kentucky where she would leave me alone. I had truly dodged that bullet.

Chapter 12

Life wasn't too bad. I sent Betty a substantial portion of my paycheck and she continued living with her parents, so I knew Jasmine was being taken care of at all times. Betty's parents were good people, especially her mother. I visited Kentucky to see Jasmine every couple months. Every time Betty brought up living together, I said that my company was scheduled to leave for the next couple of months and got out of it. Amazingly, I kept her at bay for two years with this approach.

On a routine, three-week trip out to the field, we experienced terrible weather conditions. It was the end of March and should have been warmer, but the temperature was right around freezing. This was a particularly long trip. We spent around 20 days going to various firing ranges, grenade ranges and training in 'combat town.' The engineers built an entire town located in the heart of Camp Lejeune to allow us to train on house-to-house, and room-to-room combat. We had a CIA operative demonstrate the most effective ways of entering a hostile building. This was the real shit in learning how to effectively kill the enemy. Day after day you aimed your weapon at something and knew eventually you might be aiming it at some raghead or Russian sometime in the future. The Marine Corps trains you to kill, period.

These were live-fire exercises in close proximity. As we entered the building in four-man teams, we fired on the enemy targets, while avoiding 'friendly' targets. We were timed, as reflexes and speed could determine if you lived or died in a real combat situation.

One night we were out on patrol conducting combat training against another Marine company. Our squad leader was from Trinidad and had a strong accent. He was generally a nice guy, but his sense of direction and ability to navigate a compass were truly lacking for a Marine who had reached the rank of sergeant. We made our way through thick brush and suddenly came up to water. It was all around us and there was nowhere to go besides where we came from. Sergeant Dandas was too proud to turn around and go back, so he made us all enter the water while it was thirty degrees outside, pitch black, without cloud cover.

One by one we entered the freezing water up to our chests. It felt like my chest was in a vise grip and took all of my concentration to not gasp and yell. Slowly, we made our way through two hundred yards of murky, freezing cold water. We held our rifles above our heads to keep them dry and clean. As we exited the water, the feeling of cold really set into all of us. We kept looking for 'the enemy' for the next two hours, not getting close to drying out or warming up. It absolutely sucked and all of us were pissed at Sergeant Dandas for his lack of judgment and stupidity.

The next day, Silva came up with a song that he sang all day to piss off the sergeant. We all learned the lyrics and began singing along with him. It went along with Janet Jackson's "Control" song. "Patrol... gonna get lost again. Patrol...Dandas leading us in cold, Patrol... don't know where to go." We all added more lyrics throughout the day and Dandas got more and more pissed though he never raised his voice, ever. "At ease, at ease, Marines," is all he would say.

It got closer to the end of our time out in the field. We

all stood around a fire discussing what we should do when we returned to the barracks. We were going to have a 96 (meaning 96 hours of time off), so we each started throwing ideas out about what would be fun to do. Dave blurted out that it was right around the time for spring break and that we should take a trip to Daytona Beach. It struck a chord with everyone and the idea took life. That's all we could talk about for the next few days, waiting to get back to the barracks and start our 96. The only problem was that I was scheduled to meet with the dentist the day we got back from training.

The military medical personnel sometimes performed procedures as a way to help them train, not because they needed to be done. Unfortunately for me, I had four wisdom teeth and even though they had never bothered me, the dentist decided that they needed to be removed right then. This would put a damper on anyone's plans, but as someone who was 19, there was no stopping me from going on spring break with my boys. I sat in the chair getting my teeth extracted and it wasn't too awful until the last one. The Novocain had worn off by that time and when he pulled the tooth out, I really felt it. I jumped out of the chair as he pulled it out of my mouth. Finally, it was over and he told me that I would bleed from the extracted areas for the next few days and needed to take it easy. That was not going to happen.

We had a caravan of three cars including my S-10 pickup truck loaded with three guys riding in back. Of course, they were drinking Mad Dog 20/20 and were pretty tanked within hours of our departure. My cheeks had swollen up making me look like a chipmunk. Letting Dave and Todd do the driving, I sat in the passenger seat. It took us nine hours to get there, but ten guys were ready to party and chase young college girls. None of us had the insight to call hotels ahead of time to see if they had any rooms. We began looking for a cheap place to stay and luckily, it didn't take too long to find one.

I finally felt up to driving while we were in the hotel parking lot. Todd was standing up in the back of the truck when I gunned it. Peeling out, Todd went flying out the back, landing in the dirt parking lot. I hadn't realized that he was standing up, which caused everyone to laugh as he squarely landed on his ass.

Todd, Dave and I started drinking heavily as we were so excited to have finally made it to Daytona. The town was buzzing. You could feel the electricity in the air as all of the young college students descended on Daytona to party it up for spring break. Our first trip was to the beach bar. It was jam-packed with college-aged students from all over the country. We started doing shots and talking to the girls. I could barely talk with the gauze still in my mouth and blood leaking from my wounds. It sucks tasting blood constantly; it makes it really hard to enjoy drinking, but I did my best. Within a few hours, we had some pretty attractive girls over to our hotel room. Dave asked us to give him a few minutes of privacy with his girl as things had heated up between them. We saw them making out pretty heavily just a few minutes prior to asking us to get out. We knew they were going to bang it out, as most of the girls were ready to get wild that weekend. What sucked for me was that even though the girl I was talking to was really into me, I just couldn't kiss her, knowing the foulness in my mouth. We could hear Dave going at it with his girl. The hotel didn't have air conditioning, so the windows were open. Each of us busted out laughing.

That night, the whole crew went to a bar that was

holding a huge bikini contest. There had to be over 40 girls competing and each one of them was smoking hot. Todd somehow made it up onto the backside of the stage and got the most amazing view of all the girls. I took a picture of him with the biggest grin on his face like someone who had gotten away with murder. Dave and I kept asking each of the contestants if we could oil them up to help with their onstage appearance. None of them took us up on it until finally, one did. She was amazingly hot and let us rub her fully with oil. She was very naughty, bent over and said to make sure to get her ass good, as she wanted to win the contest. We were dying as Dave and I looked at each other with shit-eating grins. Spring break was awesome. The next day we made it to the concert venue where MTV had set up their operations. We had gotten a few Budweiser cardboard guitars and were feeling pretty buzzed as we were most of that weekend. The cameras from the MTV crew turned on us and we made the most of it. Dave, Todd and I started playing air guitar and doing it up right. None of us had shirts on and we were all ripped from the training regimen the Marine Corps put us through. It was our 15 minutes of fame as they kept the cameras rolling on us. Some of our buddies who hadn't made the trip saw the coverage back at base.

The weekend sadly came and went too fast as we loaded up to head back to base. We were so lucky we were in our teens and early twenties and able to recover quickly from heavy partying.

Of course, we had PT the morning we came back from our spring break trip. Reveille was at 5:30 a.m. as usual and we were to report to formation in PT gear at 0600. Halfway through the run, each of us projectile vomited, expelling the poison of over drinking for a 96-hour period.

The funny part was that we never stopped running or missed a step as we ran in formation. The beauty of being young.

Chapter 13

Twenty-four hours a day, seven days a week, three hundred and sixty-five days a year, there is a Marine expeditionary force ready to strike any target in the world at a moment's notice. This is what it means to be on deployment. The 1st Battalion, 2nd Marines, B Company boarded the USS Guadalcanal to set off for a six-month deployment. Living on one of these ships was nothing like anything you've ever experienced. There were 20 people sleeping in a 10x10 foot area. The racks were stacked on top of each other and you couldn't turn over in your bunk without getting out first. The rack above you was less than a foot from your face. Not only that, but you had a fire extinguisher attached to the rack in your face, as well. It was pretty exciting being on deployment at first since I loved the ocean.

Unless you were on guard duty, were manning a machine gun or had mess duty, your job was to stay the hell out of the way of the Navy guys. They completely ran the ship. Whenever there was a call for general quarters, our job was to get to our racks and stay there. Needless to say, we had a lot of free time on our hands. Some of it was spent doing PT and some was spent cleaning weapons, but a great deal of time was spent fucking off. Frank, Dave and I spent a lot of time playing spades. This was by far the king game to play on the ship.

Our buddy, Troy, always seemed to catch the mess duty. With that, he would have to get up before 0500 each day to prep food. He always listened to Metallica and grew his hair out as far as he could. The platoon sergeant always had to tell him to cut his hair and because of that, he was constantly on his radar. He caught more hell than anyone else in our platoon.

Our first stop and port on our float trip was Barcelona, Spain. It was a great city and we enjoyed eight days there. We got a platoon softball team together and joined a tournament. Since we were all practically teenagers and in the best shapes of our lives, we had one badass softball team. The only problem was that I slid trying to score at home plate and gave myself a huge strawberry that was all mangled skin packed with dirt from the field. When we returned to the ship I took a shower and tried to clean up the damage, but we only had trickling water pressure and I wasn't able to clean it well. Two days later we were playing in the softball championship and being the 19-year-old dumbass that I was, I slid again. More dirt got into the wound that already didn't look good.

This time, when I went back to the ship, I visited our Navy Corpsman to show him my leg. This guy was a complete idiot and had hardly any supplies in his medical bag. He wrapped my leg with an ACE bandage and did nothing else. It didn't make much sense to me, but I wasn't an expert in first aid so I didn't question it. After a few days, I woke up one morning and couldn't even walk. Red lines came from underneath the bandage. My leg felt hot and I started to feel nervous. Crawling my way up three flights of stairs to the ship hospital, I lifted my cammies and showed the doctor my leg. His eyes almost popped out of his head! The next thing I knew, four or five people surrounded me, threw me on the hospital bed and put an IV in me. Immediately, they started scraping the wound. I jumped up out of the bed writhing in pain as they frantically worked on my leg. Only after the fact did they tell me that I was just a few hours away from losing the bottom part of my leg altogether. The head doctor asked me, "Who the hell put this ACE bandage on you?" I felt bad for the Corpsman at the time and evaded the question. Spending the next four days in the hospital, they woke me every hour on the hour to clean and redress my wound. It looked pretty grotesque with a white coating and red blood coming up through a few spots. Finally, they released me and let me get back to my guys. All of my boys came to see me while I was laid up, but it was better to be back with them instead of being tortured hourly.

You develop a routine when you live on a ship. Some people stay up and are night owls while others maintain a normal schedule. A lot of guys stayed up all night playing cards or watching porno. This one I really couldn't understand; why torture yourself? You knew when someone was going to the head, nine times out of ten it was to go whack off.

One of the guys, Melendez, was a married Marine who was so in love with his wife that I really respected him since I was in the exact opposite situation. One of his close buddies followed him to the head, put a camcorder over the stall and got him on tape spanking his monkey. Truly hilarious shit. Melendez chased Rios around the ship for days trying to get that tape. Rios kept threatening to send the tape to Melendez's wife to show her what he was up to since he'd been gone. When you're in that close of quarters you have a real bond with the guys who are going through it with you. If you have someone who is not conforming or pulling his weight then he will be dealt with by the platoon.

This happened to our Navy Corpsman, the same guy who almost caused me to lose my leg. Most Corpsmen are awesome, but our guy was pathetic. Every Marine platoon is supposed to be given a Corpsman who is attached to them. They are there to give you first aid in case you get hit on the battlefield. They are supposed to carry medical supplies in their first aid kit at all times. This guy carried Twinkies, Ho-Hos, and candy. That's all this ass clown had in his medical bag, what a fucking joke.

This, of course, contributed to him bandaging my wound up with an ACE bandage and half ass doing his job. Carrying around all that junk food, he was in terrible shape and couldn't keep up with us during PT. The worst offense that we could just not abide by was that he had terrible hygiene. He wouldn't shower around anybody else, and as such, took a lot fewer showers than everyone else. If you want to alienate yourself on a ship that was the one thing to do, not shower often. Living in such close proximity, everyone started to smell him too often.

His feet smelled like rotten fruit that had sat in the sun way too long as they fermented to the point that you could almost taste it on your tongue. All of us finally had enough and nicely let him know that things needed to change. He was going to have to get over his fear of washing his nasty ass in front of other people because we weren't going to smell him anymore. Unfortunately for him, he didn't heed our warnings and we took quick, decisive action to rectify the problem. One night when he drifted off to sleep we reached the end of our rope, sick from smelling his nastiness. Five of us jumped him and drug his ass to the shower where we proceeded to take soap and scrub brushes to him. His skin turned red from being scrubbed so hard. He screamed, "No, no!" and we needed to clean him and clean him good so that he wouldn't subject us to his nastiness anymore. Instead of just taking a shower every

day, he asked to be moved to a different birthing area.
Problem solved.

Chapter 14

The next stop on our deployment was Mombasa, Kenya. Our commanding officer scared the shit out of us by telling us this was ground zero for AIDS and that 50 percent of the population had full-blown AIDS. Every other person you met had AIDS. It was scary as hell. I doubt these numbers were accurate, but they were effective. Everybody kept their dick in their pants.

Kenya was absolutely breathtaking and beautiful. Watching elephants walk around on TV doesn't compare to watching them really walk around without anybody regulating where they walked or what they did. It takes your breath away to see nature in such a primitive way. Most people in Mombasa didn't have shoes and those that did, were someone special, very elite. It was very poor there, the poorest country I had ever visited up to that point. As soon as you come off the ship we were surrounded by villagers saying, "Come see my shop, come see my shop." What they meant by shop was a blanket that had the most amazing hand carved soapstone and wood artifacts you would ever see. The detail of these figures was amazing. We all started handing over money left and right to buy this stuff. It was so cheap compared to what it would cost in the United States that we just couldn't help it. I found out a little later in the week that bartering was the name of the game in Mombasa. Shoes were like gold over there. I actually traded my nasty Wog Day running shoes that I was going to throw away for the most beautiful, hand carved, soapstone chessboard. I would estimate the value of that chessboard to be at least $300 dollars in the US.

Dave, Frank, Todd and I went out to the local casino and played a few games. We hadn't been off the ship in quite a while so we all started to get a little drunk. Some of the locals told us about the hottest nightclub in Mombasa so we headed there. In Kenya, most people take baths only once a month and the rest of the time, rub oils on themselves to keep away the odor. As soon as we opened the door to this nightclub we were almost knocked down by the body odor that emanated, like getting punched in the face with a foul smell. We went in anyway. Young and dumb. We danced with the locals and had a pretty good time.

After a little while, I noticed Frank and Todd making their way out the door with two nasty looking females. I went into a panic. I knew what they would end up doing. '50 percent' resounded in my head. I tried to get out to stop them. By the time I made it outside they were speeding off in a cab. I grabbed Dave and we waived down a cab. Of course, I stopped the next cab and gave the infamous line, "Follow that cab!" The cab drivers in Mombasa could give the New York cabbies a run for their money. Pedestrians don't have the right of way. I could swear that these cabbies actually tried to run over a few people. My cabbie never caught up to the other cab that carried Frank, Todd and their escorts. We pulled up to where we assumed they got out and we went looking for them. Our cab driver pulled away. This was not a good part of town. It was run down mud huts and dirt roads. There were some locals just hanging around. All of them seemed to be carrying walking sticks. There was no sign of Frank or Dave. I knew they had to be in one of these huts, I just didn't know where. I started calling out for them "Frank! Dave!" I got no response. By this time, I started to notice more and more locals coming out of the shadows, starting to mass, and I started to feel a little nervous. People in Mombasa had been extremely nice to us, but I got a bad feeling. They started to surround us and I went into panic mode. I started screaming at the top of my lungs for Frank and Todd. They finally heard me and came running out of a hut.

We were all surrounded now. I would guess there were 10 guys with sticks surrounding us and looking to do us some true bodily harm. I remember thinking that if they were able to get us, we would all likely end up dead. Frank reared back and hit the Kenyan that was closest to us and grabbed his stick. It was awesome. He started swinging at the crowd. The boys and I grabbed a couple more and got their sticks. We started laying into these villagers and more and more of them started appearing. We decided to make a run for it. Though we are Marines and in phenomenal shape, these are friggin' Kenyans. The guys who win all the damn marathons in the world are chasing after us. Brilliant, huh? They stayed on our ass for a mile and a half before they finally quit pursuing us. My heart was in my throat. I truly felt we were close to death. Luckily we made it back to the ship unscathed. I bitched Frank and Todd out for being complete idiots and putting us in that situation. We had a big laugh about it later on.

After leaving Mombasa we held an amateur boxing tournament on the ship called 'smokers'. Dave and I signed up to fight other Marines and Sailors and see how we could do. I squared off against a tall Marine that had a definite reach advantage against me. The bell rang and immediately I unleashed a furious assault of punches on my opponent. I bobbed and weaved as my grandfather taught my cousins and me when we were young. This guy was no match and didn't hit me one time as I dispensed a serious beating on him. He was really tough though so finally his corner threw in the towel to stop the fight. Troy coined a nickname for me that he would call me from that moment on Mark "The Blur" Milano.

Dave got in the ring with his opponent and as soon as the bell sounded, ducked a punch and countered with a left hook that sent the Sailor straight to the floor, knocked out cold. Dave had serious boxing skills and he dispensed of his opponent fast. My entire platoon celebrated our victory and had bragging rights for quite a while on the ship.

Our Mediterranean float ended fairly abruptly when we started having trouble with the Iranians. Rebels starting taking over oil platforms that were US owned. The majority of our unit was pulled off the ship because we were too big a target for the silkworm missiles in the Persian Gulf. The USS Guadalcanal was to head into the Persian Gulf and protect our country's interests. We were taken off the ship at Diego Garcia a tiny island located directly in the middle of the Indian Ocean. After a couple of weeks there we boarded a C-5 plane and headed back to Camp Lejeune. The C-5 was the biggest plane in the world at that time and we spent nearly 19 hours without a single window to look out of. I was between Dave and Todd the whole way around the world back to Camp Lejeune. It was wild to fly around the world like that. We had a great time goofing off on the plane ride home. We were looking forward to normal American food. I guess I forgot to tell Betty that our unit had been sent back three months early. As far as she knew, I was still overseas.

Our battalion commander was pissed to not be on deployment anymore and took it out on us. He decided that our barracks became the ship; we had to pretend to still be on deployment. We weren't allowed to leave the barracks, never mind the base. Each and every day he tried to run us almost to death. Five to seven miles at a stretch at a very fast pace. This guy was hardcore; he had been shot three times in 'Nam. He could run three miles in under seventeen minutes and was a hard-charging Marine Corps motherfucker. The entire company was getting tired of running mini-marathons every day. It was getting ridiculous.

Two of my compatriots stole his running shoes when he left them out in front of his room one night, trying to get us out of running the next day. This turned out to be a monumental mistake. As we reported to formation in our normal PT attire, Lt Colonel Berger came out dressed in combat boots and shorts. This was not going to be good.

"Men, someone thought it would be funny to take my running shoes last night. Hey, I can take a joke; I am one funny motherfucker. Let's go for a run, men! I will show you how funny I can be."

As we started, each and every one of us knew we were in deep shit. He would never quit; he would run us until our dicks fell off. We proceeded to run for 12 long miles. Two-thirds of the company fell out and couldn't make it. Marines puked alongside the roadway, falling over; he set the pace so fast that most of us couldn't keep up.

We finally got liberty and a new addition to our platoon; Melvin invited us out to a biker bar off base. He had been a drill instructor but was busted for smoking marijuana on one of our surprise piss tests. He was sent back to the fleet and joined our squad, busted down to lance corporal after he had been a staff sergeant. We all liked him besides this one ass kisser corporal that gave him a hard time because of his charge. It was hilarious when the platoon sergeant asked him to march the platoon. He would get his drill instructor voice going and it was like going back in time to boot camp. "Platoon! March!" "Left, right a left!" We couldn't help, but laugh, hearing a DI's voice again.

Dave, Todd, Melvin and I made it out to his biker bar. He had built his own Harley from scratch and people at the bar knew him and made us feel welcome. They had .25 cent drafts and always roasted a pig. It was a pretty cool bar and we liked going there with Melvin. On our third trip out to the bar, there was an incident after which we would never visit again.

The four of us were outside with a number of biker guys who belonged to a biker club as they called it. We were enjoying our beers when we noticed a biker guy getting into an argument with his "old lady". None of us really paid too much attention until it escalated right in front of us. The biker lost his temper and called her a fucking cunt. Suddenly he ripped down her shorts and panties and threw her up on the truck bed. It was surreal; not one other biker paid attention to it. Melvin yelled out, "You are not doing that; that is not going to happen!" The biker looked at us, holding this poor girl down on the truck bed, and told us to mind our own business. Each one of us made quick eye contact with each other knowing we were all in and ready to fight. We made our way toward this asshole and noticed a number of bikers surround us.

We prepared to fight each one of these guys to the death and fully expected to do so. The one thing we would not allow was this fucking monster to rape his girlfriend. He finally took his hands off of her as she jumped up and quickly pulled her panties and shorts back up. I'm not sure where she went. But she quickly disappeared as the rest of us squared off, getting ready to fight. I'm sure they were used to men backing down from them, but that was not our nature and we were all ready to die right there.

The bar owner came out with a shotgun. "Everyone chill out!" No one moved or backed away. He repeated it with more force and eventually the bikers stepped back. We got in my truck and took off, never again returning to that place. We had thought that they were cool guys, but when push came to shove, they were gangsters.

Our routine for the next three months was pretty regimented because we still had to pretend we were on the ship. Our company was split apart when some of us stayed on the USS Guadalcanal and went into the Persian Gulf so they decided to transfer some of us to A Company. Todd was a short timer and due to get out of the Marines because he had done his four years.

I was one of the Marines that they transferred and was ordered to join my new platoon. It sucked to say goodbye to my buddies, especially my roommate, Frank. Dave at this time had been diagnosed with a degenerative shoulder condition and was going to be discarded on a medical. The guys I was closest to were leaving at the same time and I moved on to a new company.

Chapter 15

At the time I had been promoted to lance corporal and knew some of the guys in my new platoon. The platoon sergeant was sort of a dick, however, asked me to introduce myself to the platoon. I had been in the Marine Corps for over two years at that point. I told the guys that, "My Marine Corps name is Lance Corporal Milano, all my friends called me Mark, so you guys can call me Mark." This didn't go over well with the platoon sergeant and he had a fucking meltdown. Because that dumbass made such a big deal about it, from that point on, people called me by my first name. I met my good friend, Lamar, and his buddy Jim. They had been on a UNITAS float. This is a deployment around South America. Lamar was from Gainesville, Georgia. He was a big old country boy, 6'2" and weighed about 215 pounds. Lamar was strong and at the same time such a big kid. He wouldn't hurt a fly. He became my main drinking and chasing after girls buddy. We made up an award each week called the "dirty dog" award. This would go to the guy in the platoon that did the dirtiest sexual thing for the week, slept with the nastiest girl or some other moral breaking feat. Lamar and I usually traded this trophy on a weekly basis. We were so much alike. Jim was from Pennsylvania around six feet tall and weighed around one hundred and ninety pounds. Jim was given a couple of choices as to joining the Marine Corps. The judge he stood in front of said he could either go into the Marine Corps or go to jail for assault. He had gotten into a fight at a bar. This wasn't the only time he had been in front of this judge, so the judge thought he should try to help Jim straighten his life out and thought the Marine Corps would do the trick. Jim was absolutely crazy though.

There is nothing that this guy wouldn't do. Some guys would sit around and play chicken by lighting cigars and placing them between their arms, to see who would move first. Jim never lost and had the scars to prove it. He had one true love in his life and that was explosives. Our nickname for him was "master blaster". He always had a block of C4, a detonator cord, and blasting caps with him. Of course, this is completely illegal and he would go to jail if anyone found out.

These were some of the guys I lived with for the next two years. I was lucky and somehow ended up getting a room to myself. Usually, you shared a room with two other guys, but for some reason, I always ended up by myself. This was kind of funny because everyone would always end up in my room. I was the only guy to order cable in the barracks so my room became the party room.

I had a unique opportunity to become Water Safety Qualified because I was a very strong swimmer. It is a brutal test in the water that pushes you to your limits, but I wanted it badly. I showed up at six a.m. to go through the test. The first thing I did is get in the pool camouflage and boots on and tread water with a number of other Marines, trying to qualify. We tread water for an hour straight as the instructors threw stuff in the water at us and blasted us with fire hoses. They are supposedly simulating storm surge water conditions in the ocean, but I think they enjoyed torturing us while we desperately kept our heads above water. I was tired after doing that for an hour, but they did not delay in making us do our next swimming test. Good thing this one was easier.

We had to jump off a 50-foot platform with a full pack and swim the length of the pool. In all accounts, it was pretty simple as long as you were not afraid of heights.

Jumping from that height, the most important thing to remember is to cross your legs tight and bring the heel of your hand up against your chin while covering your nose, to protect against water shooting into your brain. Coming in the water from that height and at that speed can be dangerous if not done right. The hardest part of the test came next. The instructors lined us up on one side of the Olympic pool that was 20-feet deep on one end. They instructed us to jump in, push off the wall and swim underwater until the halfway mark. We were to surface and take one breath, but under no circumstances could our shoulders break the plane of water or we instantly failed. Then you go back underneath the water and swim to the other side, kick off the wall and resurface for one more breath. You then re-submerge and swam to the last wall. My lungs felt like they were on fire, but I would have rather died than fail that test so I toughed it out.

Almost half the guys I took the test with couldn't do it. I felt bad for my fellow students, but this is one of the hardest certifications to acquire as a Marine so I knew it wasn't going to be easy. The next step on the road to qualification was to demonstrate all of the swimming strokes down and back. The instructors then got into the pool with us. We were to rescue them and swim them across the length of the pool. Trust me, they don't make it easy. At first, they fight with you pretending to panic. It was so exhausting after going through the day of testing my limits, physically. The instructor finally went limp and felt so heavy as I had my forearm underneath his chin and most of his body supported with my side. I swam him across the pool doing the sidestroke keeping his head completely above water the entire time. I passed and was now the Company WSQ! Every time my company was near a water hazard I was called upon for duty, just waiting for the improbable occurrence of someone needing rescue.

During our downtime at the base, a bunch of us went on what would be nicknamed 'swoops' or left base and headed somewhere cool for a weekend or longer. We had a good buddy Bolyard that lived in West Virginia, near Morgantown, who always wanted us to come to his parents' house. So one weekend we decided to load up and go. It was about 550 miles from the base and we made an adventure of being on the road together. Everyone one of my buddies had some kind of craziness to them. Why would they join the Marines, otherwise? So on our trip to West Virginia, we formed a semi convoy in which three vehicles followed each other. I did most of the driving in my little S-10 pickup truck with three or four guys in the bed of the truck and three up front. I was loaded down with Marines. Driving along it started raining on my windshield though there wasn't a cloud in the sky. I looked over and one of my idiot buddies was hanging out the window of a car with his dick in his hand, pissing all over the front of my car. The guys in the back were screaming and yelling at him to put it away as they were getting the brunt of his piss. Sick fuck. Then he blew his nose into his hand and flung the snot onto my windshield. I wanted to kill him, but we were laughing too hard. We had roadies of Mad Dog 20/20 in all of the flavors. My buddies would get so mad because I wouldn't stop until I made some serious time and miles so most times they had to pee in the Mad Dog bottles or off the bed of the truck.

Once we got to Bolyard's parents' place we felt like we were invading, but his parents were so cool and welcoming. Within no time we felt part of the family. Lamar and Jim took quite a liking to Bolyard's sister, Lisa. She was really cool and very hot, so what's not to like? Lamar and I made our way to a local festival that evening in the small town and met two cute girls. We had some fun with them and it appeared that things were going well so we asked them to hang out again the next day. The two girls, Lori and Laura, invited us to come four-wheeling with them. It sounded like a blast so Lamar and I met up with them the next day. I felt a real connection with Lori and held my hands around her waist tightly as she drove us on her four-wheeler. Her body was so fit and tight; I really wanted her badly, but played it cool and didn't get too handsy. I must have liked her quite a bit. The rest of the crew was just hammered from drinking Jack Daniels and beers since we arrived. Heading to West Virginia on the weekends became routine for us and I had a hot girl that motivated me to make the trip. Many different people came along for the West Virginia trip, but it always comprised of Jim, Lamar, Bolyard, Troy and myself as the core group.

Lamar was my running buddy and we always got into some sort of trouble. One time we made our way into Morgantown, where West Virginia University is located, and one of the most fun, crazy towns and bar scenes I've ever seen. Lamar and I walked into a bar and befriended the rugby team. Those guys were as crazy as we were. All night long I told pretty college girls that I flew jets in the Marine Corps. Lamar was pissing his pants, he thought it was so funny. Shot after shot we took with the rugby guys. I noticed a cute college girl that kept making eye contact with me and decided to go talk to her. We had a great conversation and I found out she was on a marching band scholarship. Her name was Leslie; I definitely took a liking to her and she liked me as well. We were both feeling no pain as Lamar was still drinking with the rugby guys. She took her beer bottle and pulled the label off in one swipe. She turned to me and said, "I'm giving this to you." I was a bit drunk and confused so I asked her why she was giving me a beer bottle label. Leslie went on to tell me that only virgins can peel a label off a beer bottle without tearing them and that she was giving it to me. At the time I didn't take her seriously, but was too drunk to make it back to Bolyard's place, so Leslie, Lamar and I loaded up in my truck. Lamar was so drunk I had to lift him into the back of my truck as he had passed out. Lamar was no small man. Leslie took us down the street to the local motel. I put Lamar on my back and carried him into the room as Leslie opened the door for us. I threw Lamar on the bed; he fell off the side, came to rest on the floor, and didn't move until the next day. I immediately started to kiss Leslie and we made our way to the bed. We were going at it, hot and heavy. Reaching between her legs, she was absolutely soaked and wetter than any girl I had ever felt. I put a condom on and slid right inside her. She bucked and moaned loudly and after a minute or so it finally dawned on me that she wasn't lying. She was a virgin and had started to bleed all over the bed. I was pretty drunk so I was able to last quite a while before I got off. Afterwards, she snuggled up really close to me and it felt fine at the time. The next day she became really clingy, as any girl who just gave her virginity over to a guy would be, but because of the trauma I had experienced with Betty, I started to panic. I woke Lamar up and we drove her to her dorm room. The absolute shitty thing I did was give her a fake address because she wanted to write to me. I felt so awful about it later. I knew the Beast had a lot to do with why I freaked out so much. This girl was innocent and I was such a dick.

On another weekend to West Virginia, Lamar and I made our way to Morgantown to party it up again. We got there early and started looking for a bar to hang out at while we waited for our normal college bars to open. We scouted a few locations and saw some blinking lights. It looked like a bar so we went up to the door. Something was funny though; you had to ring a doorbell for some reason to get in. The name of the bar was the Double Decker. I rang the doorbell and we were buzzed in. Lamar and I walked in and asked for a drink at the bar. The bartender was about 4'10" and a stocky woman wearing interesting clothes. We decided to play pool and put quarters up on the table to get in line to play for the table. We had a few cocktails and finally, a woman stomped toward us and asked if we were next to play pool. "Yes, we are." Lamar and I headed to the back room where the pool table was and I racked the balls for this woman who was ready to kick my ass on the pool table. A guy walked up in a wife beater. This guy was huge and put his hand out to Lamar and I. "Hi, my name is Eric; what brings you boys in here tonight?" I felt so dumb right up until that point. I couldn't believe we hadn't figured out that we had found the only gay bar in Morgantown! I pulled Lamar to the side and told him; he thought I was crazy. We finished our drinks and knew we would not be meeting any girls that would have any interest, so we decided to take off. When we got back to Bolyard's place we told everyone the story of where we stumbled into and they all got a big laugh out of it.

During this time Betty resigned herself to the fact that I was constantly training and that we wouldn't be able to live together. I wasn't constantly training but wanted her to think so. I didn't want to live with the Beast; I was having way too much fun with my buddies.

Chapter 16

One day the Red Cross contacted me and this time it wasn't Betty. My CO didn't tell me anything except that I needed to get to Boston as soon as possible. My heart sank and mind raced. I rushed to the Jacksonville Airport and a plane ticket was already purchased, waiting for me. Something had happened with my father. I felt helpless and scared not knowing what was going on. He must have been in an accident or something. I anxiously took that plane ride from North Carolina to Boston. When I came out of the gate, my stepmother, Martha, was there to pick me up. Immediately I asked her what happened. She didn't say much at first, but finally, let me know that my father had cancer. I was confused. Why wouldn't they just call me and let me know this? Martha finally came out with it. He was dying and they didn't think he was going to last much longer. I couldn't believe it. I kept thinking, why hadn't anybody told me that he was sick? I am his only son. My family was like that. So self-absorbed. We waited at the airport for my sister to arrive from California and headed back to my old house I lived in before moving to Kentucky, as a teenager. Martha was a wreck so it was hard to talk to her that night.

The next morning we got the phone call; my father had passed away in his sleep during the night. Gina and I were completely stunned because we didn't even know he was dying from cancer! The pain of not being able to say goodbye when you could have had a number of opportunities to do so is excruciating. If someone, anyone in my fucking family would have spoken up, I would have been there. If I had known, I would have made time to come see him, is all that went through my head for the next few days. It consumed me.

I was in utter shock when Martha immediately started clearing out my father's closet. She threw all of his suits into a pile and started placing them into boxes. She pulled the dresser drawers open and emptied them as well. It was surreal to watch her do this right in front of me. Why the hurry? Why now?

Martha took us to downtown Boston so I could buy a suit for my father's funeral. I would have brought my dress blues but didn't know I was going to a funeral, never mind my father's. My father was a civil engineer and worked for the State of Massachusetts. He was the number two guy in charge of all the water systems for the state. I was very proud of him and looked up to him while I was growing up. I thought he was exceptionally smart and wise, though as I grew older, I felt he was controlled by Martha.

We started to make funeral arrangements, but I felt like I was in a fog. Everything happened so quickly. I felt out of control and helpless.

Somehow, Betty found out I was on emergency leave and called my father's house looking for me. I had never given her my father's phone number nor told her his full name. After she called and asked for me, I told her that my father had died, that the funeral was in two days and that I would give her a call when I got back to Camp Lejeune. I could feel her anger and irritation coming through the phone. It struck me as odd that she would be angry. Her voice had a controlling tone to it; Betty was not going to stand for this. She wanted to come up for my father's funeral and started calling to say that she was on her way to Boxford, Massachusetts. The last thing I wanted was for her to be there. I couldn't take the stress of the Beast being around and kept telling her that I would take care of things and call her when I got back to North Carolina.

Like usual she ignored me and insisted that she come up to be with me. I couldn't deal with her at this point and finally, quit talking to her on the phone. Her obsession with the phone ever prevalent, she would call every five minutes to try and 'talk'. My entire family started to feel the tension and it built every time the phone rang. I was more worried about the Beast calling and terrorizing everyone than dealing with my own grief. Martha started taking her phone calls for me. She tried to be the intervention person and calm the Beast down. The first time she talked to Betty she was very calm and nice. She tried to explain that we were dealing with this family tragedy and that she wasn't helping things by calling over and over again. It was upsetting everyone. Somehow Betty just didn't want to listen to reason and continued to call. Martha took her calls and became more upset each time. Finally, Martha told her that she would call the police in Kentucky and file a complaint against her if she called one more time. She finally got the message and didn't call again. During this time I developed a true hatred for the sound of a ringing phone, like what you see in those movies when it's all still and then suddenly the phone rings. Every frigging time the phone rang it was the Beast! I absolutely hated Betty at this time. She served no purpose than to cause me pain and heartache.

One nice thing came from the tragedy of my father's death and funeral. Gina and I got to spend time with our half-sister, Leslie, who was just three years old at the time. She was a welcome distraction. She didn't know what was going on so I spent a great deal of time playing with and entertaining her. It lightened my heart and calmed my spirit. She kept mistaking my name and calling me "Spike" instead of Mark. I thought it was adorable and stopped correcting her.

The funeral was surreal, as it hadn't really set in what had just happened. My father was highly regarded and well respected in his career so a lot of people showed up. Shortly after the funeral Gina and I were dropped off at the airport; she headed back to California and I returned to Camp Lejeune and rejoined my company.

After returning to base, my buddies took me out and we all got hammered. Just being around my buddies made me feel better and calmed me down. They were all like brothers and I leaned on them during this difficult time. I still felt so angry that I hadn't known my father was sick; it was hard to let go.

Since we were the helicopter company and flew them constantly we did some pretty in-depth training to save ourselves in case we ever crashed. We went to a massive warehouse that had a huge metal structure suspended over a 30 foot deep pool of water. It looked like a metal barrel except large enough to fit 12 people in it. The instructors told us we would be getting into this structure that was set up just like a normal helicopter on the inside.

They would drop and let us hit the water from about 30 feet up while we were in the fake helicopter. Helicopters carry all of their weight on top, as that is where the engines and propellers sit. Jim, Lamar and I loaded into the fake helicopter and were hoisted up. Just like an amusement park ride, they released us and we hit the water at full speed. Immediately the helicopter rolled over, as we held on tight while submerging underneath the water. After the helicopter went completely underwater we evacuated out of the exit doors. You have to be patient and not panic.

Each second that went by, I could see the look of some of my fellow Marines as they waited for the guys in front of them to exit the helicopter. We had two divers down in the water with us to make sure nothing tragic happened. The purpose of the exercise was to train you not to panic under the water. Tough to do when you are trapped in a metal container upside down with eighteen other guys.

Over and over we loaded into the helicopter model and changed seats so that each of us could experience the feeling of being last out and holding your breath the longest. A few times, one of the divers would have to pull a Marine out as they became disoriented and froze up. The real tricky part came when we were blindfolded with blacked-out goggles and did the same exercise. You really had to slow your heart rate, remain calm and focus on the task at hand as you were upside down underwater, trapped with eleven other guys trying to exit from two spots without being able to see a damn thing. It was a pretty intense training operation and I felt water logged from being submerged so many times throughout the day. I felt good knowing that we had all gone through it, that just in case we had to ditch in the water, we might have a chance, as slight as that might be.

One day we went out to the field. Our platoon made its way to LZ Bluebird, the closest landing zone to the barracks, to grab our ride on a CH 46 double prop helicopter. We were humping our gear and weapons as usual. I was with my normal crew: Lamar, Jim, Troy and the rest of the guys. No matter who you are, you can't help, but duck your head when you run toward a helicopter. The blades are twenty feet above your head, but you feel like they are going to take your head off each time you board one.

Everything was normal as we ran up the ramp and sat across from each other as usual. The pilot took us up and we made our way toward our training LZ. Helicopters are extremely loud and it is hard to hear anything when you are riding them. We flew for about 30 minutes when suddenly the entire helicopter went dead silent, and instantly we started free falling rapidly toward the ground. Lamar was sitting across from me and his face turned white. Each one of us knew we were going to die and panic set in on the chopper. The hardest part was not having any control over the situation; in the back of the chopper you just sit and ride it out. It is up to the pilots. In what felt like forever, they finally kicked the engines on again. A massive 53 helicopter had banked in front of us and a crash was imminent. The pilot killed the engines, saving all of our lives. It was pretty amazing, the reflexes of the helicopter pilots. The scary part is that close calls like that go on each and every day in the military.

Tony was one of my close buddies who followed me over from B Company. Previous to joining the Marines he had grown up as a cowboy. He had been part of the rodeo and ridden a number of bulls. He had the scars to go with being a rodeo guy. His face was rough and had what seemed like a full beard by two o'clock each day. He had dark hair and a black mustache. He was originally from Lebanon and had a Lebanese and American flag tattooed on each arm. Unfortunately, he had been on deployment in Lebanon when the Marine Corps barracks had been attacked by terrorists in a suicide truck that was rigged with a bomb. He didn't talk too much about it until one day when we were watching a presentation on previous military mistakes that were made. The Captain brought up Beirut and the attack on the Marines. The next thing we saw was Tony in full combat gear, standing in front of the smoldering ashes of the building the Marines were sleeping in. It was absolutely gut-wrenching knowing what he had witnessed. It gave me a whole new light on the dangers we faced serving our country as Marines.

Tony always tried to talk me into going to the country bar about 30 miles from the base. He said the older women there would just love to get ahold of me. I thought that was funny, but after a while, he wore me down and convinced me to go out with him. He had been married for a while, and he always had trouble with his wife. I thought she was kind of a bitch, to be honest. He always called her "woman", which I thought was funny. At this time they had been split up for a few months. He asked me if I knew how to two-step. "What the hell is a two-step?" Tony laughed and told me to stand up, as I was relaxing on one of the racks in the room. He slid the racks to make room. The next I knew we were across from each other holding hands in a dancing position. He gave me directions on how to two-step as I shuffled my feet, listening to his directions. We were so focused on getting my steps down, we hadn't noticed the crowd of Marines standing outside the window of the room watching us conduct what had to be one of the most amazingly funny scenes ever. They all burst out laughing at once. Tony and I whipped around and saw everyone outside laughing at us. Slowly we un-embraced from our dance. I couldn't believe I had been in that situation and for all of my buddies to see us dancing like that. We caught hell for quite a while over that scene.

I settled back into my Marine Corp life with my buddies as we prepared for another deployment. Alpha Company was due to have a six-month deployment over in Okinawa, Japan. I was considered one of the top Marines in my company and was selected to detach from my unit and join the camp guard at Camp Schwab in Japan. It is almost exactly like the MP (military police). I drove around in a Humvee and patrolled the base. When we were on duty we carried a .45-caliber semi-automatic pistol and made sure nothing illegal was going on around the base. Most Marines have a tendency to drink heavily and get a little bit out of control. A majority of my job was acting like a baby sitter.

One of the main responsibilities is to guard the armory. The Armory housed enough weapons to invade a small country. Hundreds and hundreds of M-60 machine guns, along with M-203 grenade launchers, and M-16s. It also housed grenades, LAW missiles, and explosives such as C4. It really didn't sink in, the magnitude of what I was guarding, but I was packing a shotgun and Colt .45, fully loaded with a round in the chamber.

One night I was on the Armory assignment and making my usual rounds. I spotted someone approaching my position and the Armory. We have a specific protocol to use when someone is approaching a guarded position in the Marine Corps. I initiated the protocol and said, "Halt! Who goes there?" The person approaching didn't halt or even slow down. My pulse began to raise and the hair on the back of my neck raised. Again, I demanded, "Stop! Who goes there?" Again, the figure didn't stop. I immediately reacted by racking the shotgun and running directly at the person who was disobeying my commands. My shotgun was pointed directly at his chest with my finger on the trigger, ready to take him out. "Get on the ground, get on the ground!" I screamed at him. The man immediately fell straight to the ground knowing he was in danger of being shot and killed. I put my knee down on top of his neck and pinned him to the ground as I pulled my pistol out.

"Slowly, with your left hand, reach into your pocket and pull out your ID," I commanded.

This person was in a Marine Corps uniform, but I was taking no chances at this point. He complied with my demands and I had already radioed the Sergeant of the Guard to come to my location. I checked his ID; he was a Lieutenant and told me, "I am the acting officer for guard duty this evening." He acted all pissed off at me, but I didn't care, I had followed my general orders to the letter. The Sergeant of the Guard showed up finally and I let the Lieutenant get to his feet. He kept going on about the 'trouble' I was in for putting him on his face. I gave the Sergeant of the Guard a step-by-step breakdown of the events as they unfolded earlier. He took the statement from the Lieutenant and said we would reconvene the next day. The Camp Guard reported directly to the base commander so I was summoned the next morning to speak with him. As soon as I walked into his office he walked right up to me. "Great job, Marine!" I was kind of stunned, but he told me that he was very proud of my actions and that he was going to have his boot up that Lieutenant's ass so hard he wouldn't be able to shit for a week. It was awesome to know the head of a Marine Corps base had my back and was proud of my actions. I was scared to death putting an officer down on his face like that. I thought I would be facing some serious repercussions.

I had to pull my gun one other incident during the six months I spent in Okinawa. It was a crazy incident involving a Marine who was off the base at a local bar. He was a huge, muscular guy that was absolutely tearing the bar apart. We got a call from the base commander telling us to go defuse the situation and recover the Marine. Under no circumstances were we to allow the JPs, or Japanese Police, to take him into custody. Sergeant Davis and I scrambled to the Humvee and drove as fast as possible to the Soba Bar. We rushed into the bar to retrieve the unruly Marine. As we came through the door we immediately noticed that five JPs surrounded him, and they had their nightsticks out. They were ready to give this Marine the beating of his life. Sgt Davis and I yelled at the JPs to back off; we were taking the Marine into custody. They refused to back away from their prisoner. Sgt Davis and I made eye contact, drew our weapons at the same time and pointed directly at the JPs.

"Back away from the Marine," we bellowed out.

This finally got their attention and they lowered their billy clubs. Each one stepped away from the Marine. We took Corporal Martin into custody at the risk of starting an international incident. I can't imagine what would have happened if they hadn't backed off. If there was any kind of flack from the Japanese government we never heard of it. I imagined knowing the Base Commander as I did at the time, that he ran all interference on our behalf. Especially since he gave the order to retrieve the Marine at all cost.

I knew I was lucky in landing this assignment; it was an absolute great break for me. Mentally I needed the break and loved the opportunity for six months of sleeping in a rack instead of on the ground, training.

Chapter 17

In what had to be the most disillusioned mind of all time, it finally starting dawning on the Beast that I truly didn't love her. I hadn't kissed, called, written or sent her anything on her birthday, Valentine's Day, Christmas, nothing. I was the worst boyfriend, husband, of all time on so many fronts. And I was ok with it; I felt like she had stolen something from me, forced me to live a life I hadn't chosen. She became a bit desperate and decided to call a Hail Mary, a calculated call to me at the guard shack. The whole set up was quite amazing. I could tell that something was different; as soon as I was on the phone with her she started sobbing. What now is all I could think at that time. I started to panic a bit; my heart started racing, worried at first that something was wrong with Jasmine. It was quite the opposite, by far the sweetest thing I ever heard from the Beast's lips. Truly, the best news she ever gave me.

"Mark, I've cheated on you."

Oh, she was absolutely boohooing. She was devastated, so upset, so sorry, and desperately wanted my forgiveness. It was all I could do to not jump 10 feet in the air and scream out with joy. I felt elation, what preachers must feel when they are preaching to their congregations about how the lord has lifted them, touched them, and they are free. I was so excited, I started jumping up and down and dancing all around the guard shack. The sergeant of the guard was blown away when I grabbed him and twirled him around like a ballerina. The weight that fell off of my shoulders felt amazing. The biggest smile came over my face, I can't begin to tell you how happy I was. The absolute hardest part of the entire situation was trying to remain calm through my exuberance. Patiently, I waited for her to get it all out. I knew what I would say; I had waited so long for an opportunity like this since the Beast first trapped me.

My simple reply was "Betty, I think it is best if we get a divorce." Nothing more, nothing less. This, of course, was the absolute last thing she had in mind when she called. She thought I would say that it's ok and that we need to work it out, get counseling or something. She was fucking crazy. I had waited so long, been so patient, and she had finally given me the get out of jail free card. So many times I had cheated on her, and she just didn't seem to care. Now she had given me my way out and I was going to hold on to it for dear life. She was absolutely stunned when I told her I wanted a divorce. "Wait, Mark, we need to talk," she said over and over. I couldn't hear anything. I was finally going to have my freedom! We ended the phone call with me smiling and her in disbelief; her plan backfired and I was out.

The excitement of my new found freedom would be short-lived. Betty had been dealt a blow. However, it wasn't going to stop her. This woman had put too much time in and wouldn't let me go without a fight.

In the Marine Corps. you are taught how to conduct assaults all the time when facing an enemy. The Beast created her own type of assault. She started calling me ten to fifteen times a day, every friggin' day, wanting to talk. This went on for weeks and weeks at a time. These conversations frustrated her to no end; she had lost control over me and was never going to get it back. Her voice cracked and I heard the anger and hate each time we spoke. Honestly, I tried to be nice in the initial conversations, but also remembered where that got me in the past: nowhere. I took control and put my foot down. I was not going back to giving in just because I was too much of a pushover.

Each and every conversation was the exact same; she said over and over "We need to work this out." No way, no how, was I working anything out. My time had come and I held on to it for dear life; this was my way of getting away from her for good. I could finally take a breath again, like I hadn't breathed air in years. I was suffocating and hadn't realized the extent of how oppressed she made me feel. It was so liberating, being set free. In the most firm and strong voice I had, I told her, "I don't want to talk with you anymore, Betty; please stop calling." I made it perfectly clear that I only wanted to hear from her if something was wrong with Jasmine and I needed to be consulted.

The Beast was let out and all too ready to unleash her reign of terror. This situation stoked the fire and made her exceptionally angry. She was no longer in control and I would feel her wrath. Relentless, she started calling every 15 minutes. Each time, my fellow Camp Guard Marines got me from my barracks and I had the same conversation with her. After taking a number of these calls, I told the sergeant of the guard that I didn't want to talk to her and to not bother me with her phone calls. I was adamant and deliberate in explaining to my fellow guard members that I was done speaking to my wife.

I felt blessed to be overseas when this all went down. She never, ever stopped calling. Her phone skills were amazing as she was able to convince someone to do her bidding. She would talk whoever took the call into going and getting me. I felt bad for the guy who came and got me so I ended up still taking the calls. Ever leery of her agenda and motivations, we went around in circles every phone conversation. It was a bad broken record, over and over, the same. "We need to work this out; we need to work on our marriage," is all she ever said.

I finally revealed that I never loved her, I thought she was a wacko, I couldn't stand to be around her, and my skin crawled when I think of her. I asked the Beast point blank, "Why is it, you think, that we never kissed again after I said those horrible words, I do?" It was all I could think to do to get the message across to her, though I knew it was cruel. This had no effect on her whatsoever. She was a machine, impenetrable. After finally having a serious talk with the sergeant of the guard, laying it out to him that she was harassing me, what she had put me through, and that no matter what, she wouldn't stop or give up, he understood that I wasn't going to take any more phone calls from the Beast.

Ever cunning and resourceful, this wasn't going to stop her. She had the audacity to start calling the base commander, telling him that she needed to talk with me and that I refused to talk with her. This is the head guy of the base I was stationed on. She told him how desperate the situation was and that I really needed to talk to her. The military is very regimented and has systems and procedures for everything. No one is prepared for a crazy, creative wife who becomes strategic with her battle plans and tactics, systematically putting things in motion to make people dance for her.

As a peon in the military, you never see anybody of any real rank. Your company commander is usually the highest rank you see. He is usually a captain, just above a lieutenant. You may on rare occasions see your battalion commander who happened to be a lieutenant colonel. Betty called and spoke with a two-star friggin' general. In the military, shit rolls downhill, so I'm standing at attention in front of the captain of the guard explaining why some distressed wife is calling the base commander about her personal problems. My ass was chaffed from the ripping it received, thanks to my lovely Beast, and I was told that I needed to make it my mission to communicate with my spouse. No doubt this initiative came from the top and was meant as an order.

Attempting to make my plight understood, I had a lengthy discussion about how unpredictable and unstable her actions and mindset were. After hearing my tale of woe, expecting just the slightest hint and hope of sympathy, I got, "You need to take care of it. She is your wife and your responsibility." Ouch. All I could think of was how the hell I was going to contend with this psycho. Getting my wind again, regaining my composure, I started taking her phone calls again just to appease her from doing anything else crazy. One thing was certain, I was standing firm. I was not going to stay married to her. Nothing was clearer to me in my entire life; I had to get away from her. No matter the cost, I finally stopped taking calls and attempted to make it apparent that I wouldn't cave into her again. The last thing I said in that conversation was "Do your worst, I'm not talking to you again."

The Beast took it up a notch. She decided to call the base regimental chaplain and tell him her tale of woe. Here I go again, standing at attention in front of the regimental chaplain, a very nice guy for a lieutenant in the Navy, trying to do his job. Of course, he wants to counsel me about my marriage. He had fallen prey to the Beast himself and went on to say things like, "I've had lengthy conversations with your wife and she loves you so much; you need to try and work on your marriage." I was floored. She came across so normal. She was the most down to earth and put together person to anybody she ever spoke with. The sergeant of the guard, who I happened to play racquetball with on our off days, finally came with me to one of these required meetings I had to go to and told the regimental chaplain how many times she called, and some of things she had personally said to him to get me on the phone. Finally having some credibility, the regimental chaplain let me out of mandatory 'counseling sessions.'

Once my unit returned from training in Korea I went and saw my buddies, Lamar, Jim, Troy and the rest of the guys to see how things were going. They bitched about how cold and miserable Korea was and I, of course, rubbed it in about the hot chow I got every day, along with a comfortable rack. I got a resounding "fuck off" from almost all of them. At that time I spotted my gunnery sergeant and knew what I had to do. I asked him if we could talk. He said sure and I followed him to his office. Gunny Rodriguez had recommended me for the special assignment of Camp Guard and we had a great relationship. I laid it all out to him, what had been happening, and he was in disbelief. He knew I was a standup guy and told me that he would make some calls on my behalf to cool the heat that was on me from the Beast.

Chapter 18

The sun was out and I was finally having a great day, no Beast calls. I was enjoying the sun on my face and the smell of the ocean air from the nearby beach. I wore my uniform and manned the front gate for Camp Schwab. Something caught my eye that I hadn't seen the entire time I was stationed at Okinawa, a beautiful, blonde haired girl driving up to me. Her smile mesmerized me, captivated my soul and made me stutter ever so slightly. Meeting her was like a storybook. It felt like for forever since I had seen a beautiful girl like this. She drove an absolute beater of a car. A red flag was that she was dropping off a woman she was dating. Not to be deterred by that minor detail, I stopped her on the way out the gate. Demanding flirtatiously, I told her that I simply had to know her name and where in the hell on Okinawa she came from. She simply said, "Hi, I'm Dana," and informed me that she was in the Navy.

Luckily for me, Okinawa is only 78 miles across the entire island so I knew she couldn't be too far. She worked on a base fifty miles from Camp Schwab, Kadena Airbase. Dana had the kind of smile that just lit up. I was taken with her almost immediately. With some begging and pleading, she gave me her number. I wasted little time and called her the following day. I fell hard and fast for Dana; I hadn't felt this kind of emotion as an adult. I had never believed in love at first sight, but with her, my eyes opened. The freedom of telling Betty that I didn't want to be with her allowed me to open up my heart, let my guard down, and fall in love with Dana. We became inseparable, wanting to spend every day together, every minute, from the first day we met. My routine involved getting on a bus each day down to Kadena Airbase. My new sweetheart was stationed here and nothing would stop me from spending time with her.

We were so lucky; she had a room all to herself and as two young kids we spent most of our free time there. It was a huge emotional transformation for me; my heart began to care and love someone versus feeling the anger, entrapment, and spite the Beast aroused in me. Of course, the conversation came up and I had to try and explain what I was going through, but it was almost impossible for someone who is sane to understand. With difficulty we sat down and I walked her through the entire history of what the Beast had put me through. I couldn't believe how good it felt to actually love somebody. Dana tried her best to understand, but it was difficult for someone to really believe how psychotic another could act.

The Beast kept up her calling campaign, but I was hardly even around anymore to take her calls. I spent all of my time with Dana. We loved hanging out at the beach, going for rides around the island and making love in her room. No doubt, she was my first true love.

I don't know what gave me the courage, but I finally told Betty that I had met somebody else and that I loved her so she needed to move on. Looking back now, this was a really big mistake. She set in motion Def-Con 4 and started calling the base commander again. I was again front and center, standing at attention in front of the base commander. Chills ran up my spine and I actually began to perspire in his office; sweat glistened off my forehead. Thank God he took pity on me; luckily he was an older gentleman and this wasn't his first time around the block. My gunny had intervened and made the call. This was a general who actually had compassion for me after I told him what had been going on and a little about my life. Finally, she could no longer use the Marine Corps against me; I never was bothered by anybody on that base again about Betty. Her head was about to blow off once she got the message from everyone to stop calling.

The Beast wasn't going to let a frivolous, weak-minded group like the Marines stop her. No one was going to deny her the ultimate goal. My life continued on with Dana and things grew stronger between us each and every day.

Chapter 19

Within two weeks I received a message from the Red Cross. They simply told me that Betty had attempted suicide. In my mind, all I could think is, "Oh, just attempted?" Damn. It was actually quite pathetic, her feeble attempt of suicide. She waited until her mother pulled up in the driveway and then took a total of six sleeping pills. The Beast laid the pillbox right next to her on the bed, open, with some pills out on the bed; very dramatic. Her mother was very upset, as any mother would be, and rushed her to the hospital. They immediately pumped her stomach and released her the next day.

Everyone expected me to take emergency leave to go take care of that psycho because we were married. But they didn't know the story of what had gone on, what she had been putting me through. When it got right down to it, I didn't want to go on emergency leave. I was happy staying in Okinawa with Dana, the girl I truly loved. The Beast was determined to get me to come home and the one factor that finally made me decide to do so was my daughter; she weighed heavily on my mind at this point. If Betty was willing to do this to try and get attention, what else would she try? Could I leave Jasmine in Betty's hands, as unstable as she was? The only comfort was that Betty's mother was there to look after and take care of Jasmine. I knew she wouldn't allow Betty to harm Jasmine. I have to admit that I never feared Betty harming Jasmine up to that point, but now I knew she was fully capable of harming me, herself.

Things were like a whirlwind that day. After all of that craziness, I finally talked with Betty on the phone. It was extremely hard to hide the anger and hatred I felt for her at this point. What was she thinking? Why did she do this? Even though it didn't matter she started the whole thing in so many ways, quitting school, not taking the hint so many times that I didn't want to be with her, getting pregnant on purpose and finally stating that she had cheated on me. Calmly, well, as calmly as possible, I told her that I would fly home and help her deal with her issues, for my daughter's sake. The caveat to all of this was that we were going to meet with an attorney, she needed to meet with a counselor, and we were not going to stay married. It's over, and she is going to have to deal with it. Begging me, she said a number of times, yes, we can meet with an attorney and get an amicable divorce. Just come home and help, just come home and help her. Before getting off the phone I made her swear on Jasmine's life, probably a bad move in the unstable state Betty was in, but she said, "I swear on Jasmine's life that I promise, that I understand, that we are getting a divorce and are meeting with an attorney once you get here." Of course, I remembered back to a number of her promises, "Yes, I'm still on the pill." "If things don't work out, we can stay friends and raise our daughter." I knew my journey back to Kentucky was going to be fraught with peril, and I had a sneaking suspicion that we weren't going to stay friends like she promised we would be if things "didn't work out, per se."

At that time I really knew that I loved Dana and had started telling her as much. I reassured her that I would be back soon. She was afraid that I would go back to Kentucky and work things out with Betty. That had to be the last thing in the world I would ever possibly do, but she is a woman, and they have those fears on occasion. I expressed my total devotion to her and boarded the plane back to the United States. After a mind-numbing, 23 hour flight, I finally touched down in Lexington, Kentucky. There she was, to pick me up from the airport. Anger started swelling inside me; I couldn't help, but tell her, "What the hell were you thinking? We have a daughter that needs her mother; how could you be so selfish?" The pit I felt in my stomach, just being around her, was enormous and dark. My stomach kept turning every second I had to spend with her.

I regained control and after my initial outburst didn't say much more to her on the car ride home to Lawrenceburg. A tense silence filled the air. I was so ready to get this week over with and start my life, fresh and new. Lawrenceburg is about 25 miles from Lexington. The car ride felt as long as the 23 hour flight I had just taken. We finally pulled up into the driveway and made our way in the door. I noticed that nobody was home. Kind of made me feel a bit uneasy, to say the least, was she going to kill me? We went inside the bedroom and the next thing I knew she started to make sexual advances towards me. Horror, it was the most repulsing experience I had ever felt. My skin started crawling, my heart started racing, and not in the good way. Even as the horniest twenty something kid I could never, ever fuck her again. I pushed her away from me and told her that it was over. I didn't love her. I never loved her and she needed help. I loved Dana and told the Beast straight out as much. This didn't go over too well.

She dropped the hammer on me.

"Mark, we need to work things out, we need to work on our marriage."

I couldn't believe it. I've been told the definition of insanity is doing the same thing over and over again and expecting a different result.-She was insane. Stupidly, I asked her if she had scheduled the appointment with the attorney, like she promised, so I would come back to Kentucky in the first place. Of course not! She wanted to work things out and was bound and determined to do so. Why would we want to see a divorce attorney? At this point, I completely lost it. I had just flown 23 hours to help the mother of my daughter get her shit together, start healing and becoming normal. It was hard for me to even get on that plane in the first place because I truly couldn't stand her. Everything was a big fat lie, agreeing to meet with an attorney, agreeing to meet with a counselor and us being amicable. The whole thing was a setup from the get-go. Even the pills she took, I found out wasn't even close to a dangerous dosage to cause her any harm. My neck got hot, my eyes turned red, I had to get out of there. I truly felt like I could have killed her at that moment and was scared that I might do something to her if I didn't leave, and leave quickly. She tried to get in my way, but I side-stepped her and made my way out the door.

I walked over to my buddy, Scottie's, house. Scottie and I had gone to high school together and we from the same neighborhood. He knew Betty and I. Scottie hadn't seen me in a while, but could definitely tell I was upset. I told him what I was doing there and he couldn't believe it, any part of it. Betty had an incredible talent of acting entirely sane around everyone possible. He said, "No way is she doing those kinds of things." I just told him I flew 23 hours to get here and she had made the whole thing up, just to get me here. Betty had that kind of control over people; she made them think she was the most wonderful person in the world.

After a while, I finally calmed down and knew exactly what I was going to do. I would go back to Betty's parent's house and calmly talk some sense into her. As I entered the house again I took a deep breath ready to take this challenge of convincing her to do the right thing. I began to speak, but she interrupted me saying "you are not going anywhere." I thought that was a bizarre statement, but come to find out the Beast had been up to some astonishing things while I was out cooling off from her web of lies. She had gone through my luggage and found my 900 dollar, non-refundable plane ticket back to Okinawa. "Mark, what are you thinking?" She threw away, actually flushed, my plane ticket down the toilet. And, because she didn't want my plane ticket to get lonely on its long journey down the sewer lines, she had my military ID and emergency leave orders, stating what I was doing in Kentucky. Lovely; she was absolutely out of her damn mind. I was stuck. No way was Mark going anywhere now; she was gonna wear me down until she had me under control again. Put some kind of crazy voodoo on me; make me bend to her will.

The Beast had me, or so she thought. So many things motivated me to get away from her at that time, an absolute rage that she did that and put me in jeopardy of being AWOL. I needed to stop the churning of my stomach from being around her, and get back to Dana. I was so tired of the Beast controlling so many aspects of my life like she had for so long. No one was going to do that to me ever again. It was time for me to get control, so I grabbed my suitcase and walked out the door of her parents' house without looking back.

One step after the next, I began my 25 mile walk to Lexington in full uniform, carrying a suitcase. Betty wasn't going to give up though; she followed behind me in the car. The scene had to be unbelievable to anyone driving by.

Here was a man in a military uniform, walking along with a suitcase. Following behind, a psychotic in a truck, with her head hanging out the window yelling, "Mark, get in the car!" She followed behind me the entire way, trying to get me to get into the truck. "Mark, get in the car," is all I heard, over and over, but I knew what that meant, going back to her parents' and 'working things out.' She stayed behind me the entire trip, relentless. There was no way I was getting in that truck. The desperation and anxiety she forced me to endure, just being around her, felt like the weight of an elephant on my chest. My desperation to get away from her was self-preservation at its best. At that time I would have walked through fire, on top of broken glass, with bare feet, to get away from her. It took me about four hours to reach Lexington with Betty in tow. The only concern I really had was that she would snap and run me over so I couldn't walk anymore.

Along the way, a number of people pulled over and offered assistance. As soon as they pulled over and asked me if I needed help, the Beast would rear her ugly head, jump out of the truck and start freaking out on the innocent do-gooder. They had no idea who they were going up against in offering help. Thinking like a Marine, I headed to the only place I knew of where somebody might be able to help me, the military reserve station in Lexington.

When I walked into the reserve station I was exhausted. Even though I was in excellent shape, I was still spent from the walk, fending Betty off for 25 miles, listening to her to go on and on for me to get in the car. I had just flown halfway around the world to get to Kentucky, and now, I was desperate to leave. Getting back to Japan was all I wanted to do. I walked in and told the sergeant in the office that he has no reason to believe me, but that I was a Marine on emergency leave and didn't have an ID, my plane ticket or my emergency leave orders. I told him as much information as I could muster at that point, and he went and talked to the reserve station commander.

The commander came in to talk with me and I told him some of the story. I didn't tell him everything that had happened because I was extremely embarrassed with the way Betty was acting. She waited outside in the parking lot like a predator stalking her prey. She was going to do whatever she had to do to make me stay in Kentucky. I went outside to get some air while the sergeant started making some phone calls to see if they could help me get back to Okinawa. At this point, Betty dashed into the reserve station and stayed in there for about 30 minutes. The next thing I knew, I felt a hand on my shoulder. It was the reserve station commander. Stunned, I felt unbelievable fear. I had no idea what kind of bullshit Betty had told him. I knew she was capable of anything at that moment.

"Son, I've just had a long talk with your wife and I think it would be better if you attached yourself to my unit, temporarily, so you can work things out with your wife. She loves you," he said.

I felt like I was hit with a sledgehammer. It knocked the wind out of me. How is she pulling this off? I had to shake it off, recover and stop my head from spinning. "Get back in the game, Mark," I kept telling myself. I told him that I really appreciated the offer, however I just wanted to get back to Okinawa. I never wanted to leave the United States so badly in my entire life. He finally said that it was my choice and that they would help me. I thought he was going to use his rank to influence my decision and make me stay there with Betty. I felt like I had dodged a major bullet. They made all the necessary phone calls and found out I was who I said I was.

They issued me a military ID card issued and worked out a deal to take money out of my check for the next year to pay for the plane ticket back to Okinawa. I didn't care at that point; I just wanted to get away from Betty. One of the reservists gave me a ride to the airport. The Beast was in full pursuit and followed right behind us. The airport was only 10 minutes from the reserve station. I had no idea what she was up to next. A lot of anxiety and fear started taking over me as she followed behind. Each minute that went by I knew she might get more and more desperate.

Slowly, we pulled up to the airport and he dropped me off. As I opened up the passenger door, I saw the Beast pull right up behind us. She just left the truck there and followed me into the airport. She grabbed my arm a number of times so I would stop to talk to her, but I was a man on a mission, to get the hell out of Dodge. She stayed right next to me as I went to the ticket counter and got my ticket to California; I would catch another plane back to Okinawa from there. Holding that ticket in my hands, I started to feel the slightest bit of relief that I would get away from her. I put a serious kung fu death grip on that ticket because I knew Betty would rip it out of my hands if given the opportunity. That crazy bitch would have burned it on the spot if she could have gotten her hands on it.

I start making my way toward the gate area. She followed me all the way to the gate, talking to me the entire way. She said everything possible to get me to stay. "Mark, we need to work this out; do it for Jasmine's sake." I just blocked her out and kept walking. We finally reached the gate area. There were a number of other gates in the immediate vicinity, and hundreds of people were going about their business, waiting for their planes. The Beast spoke in circles, over and over, the same mantra. She was like a sick, demented record. "You can't leave; we need to work this out." Her pitch grew more and more desperate. I just tuned it out.

Waiting for the announcement to board the plane was agonizingly long and painful. Like a gift from God, they finally called my flight! Betty's demeanor changed; a darkness took over as she knew I was actually leaving and there wasn't a damn thing she could do about it. My heart raced; I was excited to be leaving; I knew that Betty would be on a path of destruction from that point forward. Taking the first steps I started making my way across the terminal toward the gate. All of a sudden, Betty leaped at me, Superman style. She flew through the air, grabbed me around my waist, slowly slid down to my ankle and locked down on my leg. She felt like a pit bull clamping down on my ankle with crazy strength. I was absolutely shocked that she was actually lying on the floor in the middle of the airport terminal, wrapped around my ankle. Everyone, and I mean everyone, stopped what they were doing; you could hear a pin drop in the gate area. Horrified and stunned, people just stared silently at the spectacle. Mouths dropped to the floor, children pointed. My face was flush; I had never been so embarrassed in my entire life. She wasn't letting go, either. And no way in hell was I going to reach down and touch her.

Nothing was going to stop me; I was determined to get on that flight, and no way was she going to mess it up. I started dragging her across the terminal toward the gate, one step at a time. One step forward, then pull my leg up to the next one, pulling her along. Her body rubbed against the airport carpet, making a friction sound each time I pulled my leg forward. With everyone silent that is the only sound you could hear in the gate area, the sound of her scraping against the carpet. At the time, she had psycho crazy strength, no chance of letting go. I just kept going as everyone watched the astonishing ordeal.

Finally, after dragging her 40 feet through the terminal, with everyone in the world watching, and it felt like a fucking eternity, I reached the flight attendant. A little breathless, and panting a bit, I handed over my ticket to freedom. The flight attendant looked down at the Beast strapped to my leg, clutching for dear life. Betty wouldn't even look up and make eye contact with anyone. She finally showed her true, crazy nature to the world. The flight attendant came around from her desk, leaned over and ever so calmly said, "Miss, you can't get on the plane without a boarding pass." It was classic, looking around and seeing the stunned faces of all the spectators watching this incredibly embarrassing moment burnt in my mind. It took three security guards to finally break the Beast's grip and remove her from my leg. As I left, I didn't say a word to her. I felt contempt and disgust for her. Getting on the plane, I felt everyone's stare. I felt like a circus freak. After getting on that plane, I avoided eye contact with every single person on the flight. I knew at that point that I had a true psychopath to contend with. She was going to be the most dangerous person I have ever contended with in my entire life.

I was definitely relieved when the plane pulled back from the gate. My heart raced the entire time, waiting for Betty to cause another scene at the airport and somehow, someway, stop the flight from leaving. I was convinced that the airplane door was going to open up at any time and she would get on the plane. My heart palpitated until we finally pulled away.

The flight to Cincinnati from Lexington was only 35 minutes in the air. When the plane touched down and arrived, I disembarked. Finally, I had started to calm down just a little bit and had gotten some control of my emotions and the ordeal I had just gone through. I started hearing something throughout the airport, something that made my anxiety spike. I heard my name getting paged.

"Mark Milano, pick up the white courtesy phone, Mark Milano, pick up the white courtesy phone," came over the PA.

In a panic, with my heart pounding, sweat started coming out of my pores. I reluctantly picked up the phone and, of course, it was the Beast.

"Stay right there! I'll be there in an hour to pick you up. You're not going back to Japan!"

"Can she get here and stop me?" Quickly slamming the phone down, as if it were on fire, I ran to the flight information sign with straight panic and fear, hoping upon hope that my flight would be gone before an hour. I looked up on the screen, checked when my connecting flight left Cincinnati, and felt absolute relief to see that the flight left in 45 minutes. Unless Betty was willing to drive 100 miles an hour, I was relatively confident there would be no way she could get to Cincinnati and confront me again at the airport.

A huge weight fell off my shoulders as I boarded my plane to St. Louis. As we touched down, I got off the plane and heard the damn page again. "Mark Milano, pick up the white courtesy phone. Mark Milano, pick up the white courtesy phone."

At this point I was an idiot for picking up the phone, however out of sheer, morbid curiosity, I picked it up. Why in the hell I kept picking up that phone, I have no idea. I guess it was fear of the unknown. Not knowing what Betty might do next is probably what made me grab for that damn white courtesy phone. I picked it up and the Beast was on the line, of course, telling me to stay right there and that she will be in St. Louis in four hours to get me. Betty had completely lost touch with reality at this point. I was almost tempted to torture her and tell her ok, I will wait here for you, just so she would make that long ass trip to St. Louis and find me gone. It would have been classic, but my brain doesn't work as twisted and fucked up as the Beast's. I got on my connecting flight to LAX. Bracing for the page in LA, it didn't come.

The sweet sound of not hearing my name on the airport pager was music to my ears. I found the military liaison at LAX and he arranged transportation to Camp Pendleton. The next couple of days I spent in Camp Pendleton, waiting for a military flight back to Okinawa. For the most part, my days were pretty uneventful. I woke up, went to the chow hall and hung out. Finally, I boarded a plane with a bunch of new military people who were on their way to their first duty station. It was kind of nice because they were all asking me about Okinawa and what it was like to be out in the fleet. This is a term used for Marines. It means to be a working part of the Marine Corps. Instead of being in boot camp or at school, you actually have a mission that your unit is on at all times, like being on a deployment to Okinawa, Japan. I liked the attention and felt like a big shot for a little while. I had a number of medals and ribbons on my uniform at this point in my military career so they all looked up to me. It was a nice distraction from what had just happened two days earlier.

I knew it was far from over with Betty. She had shown her cards and the elevator didn't go to the top with her. I also knew she was capable of anything. Lying, cheating, and stealing, whatever she needed to do to get what she wanted. For the life of me, I just couldn't figure out why. I hadn't done anything for her to be this obsessed with me. In my entire life, I had never dealt with a situation like this and I had no clue what was in store for me.

The day finally came for me to get on the flight back to Okinawa and I was more than ready. I was so happy when that plane touched down at Kadena Airbase in Okinawa. Immediately, I made my way right to Dana. I wasn't due back to Camp Schwab for a few days and I wasn't going to spend one-second longer without her. My heart filled again as I put my arms around her and held her tight against my body. Nothing could have felt better than just holding her in my arms. Everything that I had been through in the past week had been a nightmare, and it was all over now. Over the next few days, I was able to breathe again. It was night and day spending time with Dana, compared to Betty. One felt like living through hell, and the other was peace and serenity. In my mind, the worst was over, but unfortunately, the Beast had different ideas for me.

The time came when I needed to report back to Camp Schwab and get back to my military responsibilities. I came into the guard office, checked in with the sergeant of the guard and told him a little bit about what happened. He just shook his head in disbelief. The good thing was that I didn't expect to be taking calls from Betty anymore. Her calling campaign had run up her parents' phone bill to $1,900 dollars in just over a month. Her obsession finally came back to bite her in the ass. No way could her parents afford to pay a bill like that, so the phone was shut off for a couple of weeks. Ever resourceful, Betty convinced her sister to allow the phone bill to be switched into her name and started making calls again. She convinced her sister by saying that her parents needed the phone on due to her father's health, however, Betty had only one objective in mind, and that was to call me and get me to change my mind.

They tried to stop her, but there was no stopping the Beast. The poor guys at the guard shack had to take all the calls and tell her that I wasn't taking calls from her anymore. They had to listen to her try and convince them how much of an emergency it was and that she really needed to speak with me this time. It was unbelievable how relentless she was. At the time, I felt really bad for my fellow camp guards, but they were actually having a great time with it. A number of guys had started creating pools on how many times she would call, how long would she keep someone on a call and what was the craziest excuse she would give to speak with me. They were having a blast. She tried to call everyone she could think of on the base to get somebody to listen to her, but by that time, people around the base had caught on to her antics and didn't take her seriously.

Almost all of my paycheck was being sent to Betty to take care of Jasmine. She was sent a check on the first and the fifteenth every month. When I came over to Okinawa, I set it up so that I would receive $80 dollars each payday. Most of the money was spent going out with Dana and buying stuff at the PX. Simple things like shaving cream, razors, toothpaste, stuff like that. At the PX, I was writing checks for $10 and $20 dollars each payday. There weren't any ATMs over in Okinawa that were attached to my credit union, so this is how I got cash.

I underestimated Betty's fury and hatred, as hard as that is to believe. Unbeknownst to me, Betty had called my credit union and transferred all of my money each payday, having it sent to herself. She was getting almost every penny I had anyway but wanted to hurt me in any way she could. The Beast was one vindictive bitch. She didn't want me to have one penny, not a dime. Unfortunately for me, there was a 45 day turnaround time on checks cashed overseas like that, and I had no idea she had been doing this.

The day finally came when the checks started coming back, bouncing left and right. I was absolutely floored. Almost all of my money had gone to Betty and I had no way of fixing the problem. No one prepares you for that kind of crazy. I immediately stopped my direct deposit to my account at the credit union but knew that I had at least 15 other checks out there that were going to bounce. Anger swelled in me, and my hatred for Betty grew hotter and darker. Luckily at that point, she wasn't anywhere near me or I might have tried to kill her. Writing bad checks in the military will get rank taken away from you and ruin your military career; they don't fuck around with that kind of shit.

Dana stepped up and bailed me out. She used almost every dollar of her paycheck and paid off all the checks that I had written as well as the fees. Never in my life was I indebted to someone or as grateful. Dana single-handedly saved my ass, and came through for me when my back was against the wall. I was crazy about her anyway, but this just made me feel that somebody was finally on my side. Somebody finally loved me and showed it to me in a way I could never forget. This solidified my feelings for her and no matter what our future held, she would always hold a spot in my heart.

If I could have somehow, someway reached through the phone I would have strangled Betty. She told me straight out that she wanted to make me suffer and would do anything in her power to make it happen. Financially, physically, emotionally, whatever way she could make me suffer, she would. At least she warned me and kept me on my toes.

I knew in my soul that I was in for a lot of battles ahead. She decided that if I wasn't going to be with her then she would do everything imaginable to make my life a living hell.

Over the next few months, I strategically avoided talking to Betty on the phone. In my mind, I thought if we didn't talk, she wouldn't have anything to be mad at me about. Dana and I settled into a sweet, loving, normal relationship and for the first time in a long time, I felt normal.

During one of my off days that Dana had to work, I went and saw some of my buddies from my company. They had been over in the Philippines training. Lamar couldn't believe I had gone back to the United States on emergency leave. I told him the full story. He told me I needed to stay clear of that crazy bitch. "Duh, Lamar, tell me something I don't know." It felt great to see the guys. A big group of my friends huddled around my buddy Jim; he was doing his crazy shit as usual. I think it is hard for civilians to really understand the mentality of the men and women that serve in the armed forces, especially Marines.

We were so twisted; we did the craziest things imaginable. Scofield bet Jim $200 dollars that he couldn't jack off and blow his load within five minutes with everyone was watching. Jim was not going to back down from this challenge and, of course, agreed to the bet. There must have been 20 or so guys around as Jim unbuttoned his camouflage pants, whipped his dick out in front of everyone and started stroking. He closed his eyes and tried desperately to tune all of us out as we started making comments. "Damn, Jim, that is the smallest dick I've ever seen! Hey, do you think your mother would approve of your actions right now?" We did anything we could to throw him off and stop him from the task at hand, but that sick bastard was able to get off. He actually yelled out, "Oh yeah!" as he started to cum. He tried to chase everyone around, pointing his dick at the guys giving him shit while he was taking on the task. It was like a grenade went off, each one of us ran for our lives to get away from him. Jim was one twisted individual, but he won his bet. This was the kind of craziness that went on all the time in the Marine Corps.

In fact, Lamar showed me his 'special' towel that he had been working on the whole time our Company was stationed in Okinawa. By special, I mean he had been jerking off into it and not washed it the entire time. It was discolored and stiff as a board. Lamar actually took pride in the work he put into making his biological science experiment. These were my buddies.

Not everything was perfect in Okinawa. As most young men have a lot of testosterone flowing through their veins we would have some occasional conflicts. A fellow guard and I would get together and play basketball. His name was Corporal Jones, he was tall, about 6'3" and fairly lean, but not skinny. Jones was black and he was so smooth handling the basketball I was in awe. He would bounce the ball behind his back, between his legs with absolutely no effort, it was flawless.

I wasn't a bad basketball player as I use to play almost

every day when I was living with the Michaels in High School, but this guy was way out of my league. He would stay on me about dribbling with my left hand and really helped me improve my game. Needless to say, we grew pretty close.

One day another guard named Lance Corporal Duke came and asked to talk to me. We went into the barracks area and he said he just had a confrontation with a fellow guard. I asked him what happened.

"Jones turned me in for relieving him an hour late," he said.

He had overslept and Jones had called into the Sgt of the Guard to ask where his relief was. In my mind I thought that was completely reasonable so I didn't know why Duke was so pissed. The next thing out of his mouth almost floored me.

"I want to go kill that nigger, come with me and let's go get that nigger!"

Nothing could have shocked me more as I hadn't really experienced any type of racism like that since I had been in the Marines. "Fuck you asshole, you racist fuck" is what I responded with. Duke countered with "are you some sort of nigger lover?"

I'm enraged now and wanted to beat his ass bad "come outside and let's settle this asshole." We made our way outside and no one was around to stop this and that's exactly what both of us wanted at the time. I could see that absolute hate in his eyes and he was going to take it out on me the anger he had for Jones. Fine by me is all I could think. We instantly engaged and it was within seconds that he really wished he hadn't tangled with me. I was much faster, stronger and meaner than he was. I rained down a number of thunderous punches on him. You could hear the thud of each time as the punches reached his face, he began to collapse. I crawled on top of him and hit him a few more times while he was stretched out on the grass. Finally realizing that he was beat and beat bad I regained my composure and stopped pummeling him. He wasn't knocked out so I knew he was okay, but he definitely didn't want to engage anymore.

I left him there on the ground and made my way back into the barracks. Of all people, Jones saw me come in and saw I was a bit gassed from the fight I had just been in. "What the hell happened to you?" I told him the story and he couldn't believe it, he said I should have let Duke come try and fight him.

"Sorry brother, he pissed me off and I needed to give him that beating," I said.

The next day we had formation and let's just say Duke looked awful, his face was swollen and he had two black eyes. I started to get nervous as the Captain came to inspect us to make sure our uniforms were squared away.

"What the holy hell happened to you Duke?" the Captain asked.

I got a huge pit in my stomach as I had no idea what Duke was going to say. Surprisingly Duke said "Corporal Milano and I were practicing some hand to hand combat training." I couldn't believe this racist fuck just covered both of our asses. Maybe he learned something from our altercation is all I could think.

Chapter 20

Unfortunately for me the day finally arrived; we were leaving Okinawa. It was time for me to say goodbye to Dana, rejoin my company, and head back to Camp Lejeune, North Carolina. It was heartbreaking to leave Dana behind, but there wasn't anything we could do. We were both in the military; I had to return to the US and she had to serve at Kadena Airbase for the next two years. We promised to wait for each other and make things work. I meant it. I truly loved her and would have waited for her to get back to the United States. Unfortunately, though, this was not meant to be. Within a few months, she met someone else and actually got married. I was shocked and it took me a while to get over it. This was my first real heartbreak, but fortunately I was young and able to move past it. And I always had Betty, who didn't allow me to stay distracted for too long. She was constantly barraging me with problems that I had to dig myself out of.

Alpha Company arrived back to Camp Lejeune and we began moving our stuff into our new barracks. As usual, I was on the third floor and just so happened to have a room to myself again. It was nice to be back in the United States. You don't know how much you miss things until you've been away for a while. We had been home for maybe an hour when I finished putting up my stuff and getting my room situated. All of a sudden, "Knock, knock, knock!" sounded on my door. I figured it was Lamar wanting to go to chow. No, the farthest thing from a friendly face, standing in my doorway at the barracks was the Beast! My jaw hit the floor in total disbelief.

"What the fuck are you doing here!" is all I could say.

"We need to talk," she said.

I could not believe my nightmare was starting already. Not even one fucking day back and this psycho shows up at my barracks. She had left Jasmine down in the truck in the parking lot. I was so pissed about that because Jasmine was only three years old. My face flushed and I felt like I had been hit with a sledgehammer. The Beast definitely got the drop on me. I informed her that she was not allowed at the barracks, walked her down to the parking lot and told her to leave.

She said she wasn't going anywhere until we talked. We had spoken a million times by that point. What in the world did she think would be solved now? I walked back to my barracks; she grabbed Jasmine out of the truck and started yelling at me. It was horrifying. Screaming at the top of her lungs like a complete psycho. She called me a bastard and said that she would make me pay. One by one, my buddies came out on the catwalk to see what the hell was going on. Women weren't allowed near the barracks so she had drawn quite a crowd with her obscene tirade. Panic started to hit me, as I had no idea how to handle this situation. My chest grew tight and my breath was shallow as my head started spinning. I finally got tired of her cussing and making a complete ass of herself and went back down to the parking lot to try and calm her down. I couldn't believe she had Jasmine with her while she was doing this. Why hadn't I anticipated this? How could her mother allow Betty to take Jasmine and drive down to Camp Lejeune, knowing what Betty and I had been going through? Well, that was just it. Her mother had no idea that Betty and I were having any problems. Betty told her the phone bill was so large because we missed each other so much that we had to talk to each other 10 times a day. She had been able to hide her behavior from her own parents. Betty told her mother that I really wanted to see her and Jasmine and that she would be gone for about a week.

In order to fund her little trip, Betty had gone to the pawnshop with every stereo, VCR, and TV that I owned, got as much money as she could put together and headed to Camp Lejeune with Jasmine. Each military base usually has a base hotel set up for families of military people and most times is fairly cheap. Down in the parking lot, I told Betty I would come talk with her if she would just go back to the hotel. Trying to get my bearings after being stunned like that, I told her I would meet her over there in a half hour. Taking deep breaths and forcing myself to calm down, I made my way to the hotel. Walking over, my mind raced and I didn't know how I was going to deal with the Beast. I really had no idea.

When I got to the hotel I looked at my truck in the parking lot. Something was wrong, so I went up to look at my car and noticed that she had sliced the tires on the truck. The Beast had sliced all four of them and they were not going to be fixed with a patch. They were ruined, and as far as she was concerned, she wasn't going anywhere. "Fucking crazy bitch," ran through my mind. Dreading what was in store for me, I knocked on the hotel door and she opened it up. As calmly as possible, I asked her again what she was doing in Camp Lejeune. Even knowing that I had a girlfriend that I loved, that I never wanted to be married to her, and after running for my life to get away from her a few months ago, she said that we needed to work things out. After all the crazy stuff that had happened, she still had delusions that we would stay together. I tried to stay calm because my daughter was right there in the

147

room with us, but it was hard. I tried to talk to her reasonably. I said that I wasn't happy, I had never been in love with her and that she deserved somebody that would love her.

Though, what crazy bastard would ever be fool enough to love this crazy bitch? It took every ounce of my sanity to not snap, so I tried to speak as calmly as possible, but it just didn't register with her; I just wasn't getting through. We kept going in circles about how we needed to keep our marriage together. As plainly as possible I told her there was no marriage.

After going around and around with her for hours I finally just got tired of trying to talk to with her anymore and decided to leave. Desperate as usual for me not to leave, she jumped to the floor and lay down in front of the doorway. I had never imagined someone doing something like this; she decided that she wouldn't let me leave. I felt trapped, like a caged animal. I couldn't believe she was lying down in front of the door. Who would think of something like that? I didn't want to get physical with her, especially with Jasmine there. I was trapped. I ended up staying there for an additional three more hours, talking about the same things we always talked about ad nauseam. She felt that she could outlast me, wear me down, and make me bend to her will. After promising that we would continue our conversation the next day, she finally allowed me to leave and I made it back to the barracks.

The next 10 days she stayed on the base and tried to convince me over and over to make our marriage work. It was the same routine every fucking day; I would go to formation, do my Marine training with my platoon and then be cut loose for the evening. Each day she waited for my company to be relieved for liberty and then showed up with Jasmine. The Beast had no shame and would start making a complete ass of herself to get my attention. She would have made a great interrogator for any third world country open to using torture techniques.

Numerous times she yelled while standing directly in front of the barracks, "Mark Milano is a piece of shit and doesn't take care of his daughter or his wife!" Of course, I would give in and go with her back to the hotel to talk. I went into a zone each time as I tried to keep my sanity and not snap on her. I know exactly how they came up with the expression 'trying to talk to a brick wall." Nothing penetrated her thick skull. One thing I did know, she only had so much money and eventually would run out so I just tried to wait her out.

Somebody must have been looking out for me because I had given up my seat on a flight during the previous Thanksgiving holiday. Because I did this, Delta airline had given me a round trip ticket voucher to anywhere in the US. I saw it in my locker at the barracks and it dawned on me how I was going to get out of this situation, how I would get her back to Kentucky with my daughter. The day finally came when she ran completely out of money. It was a Friday and she had to check out of the hotel with Jasmine.

In what I wanted to be my last conversation with her, I gave her $20 dollars to take a cab to the airport, handed her the plane ticket voucher and told her to take Jasmine back to Kentucky. I really needed a break from her craziness and decided I was going to Georgia with my buddy Lamar for the weekend. The Beast was absolutely stunned and for the first time in a while, speechless. I thought she knew that she didn't have any other option. I wasn't going to give her any money to stay at the hotel and torture me every day like she had been. She was going to have to go home. After 10 long days, I was finally going to be rid of her.

Lamar and I got into his truck to leave for the weekend. However, the Beast was lurking, and out of nowhere, came up to Lamar's truck and banged on the window. We both jumped at the force in which she hit the window. I thought a rock had somehow hit it; it was so loud, it actually vibrated. It scared me to death. There she was, her eyes filled with rage. Cautiously, I rolled down my window.

"Betty, you need to take Jasmine, go to the airport and go home."

She saw red and reached through the window. All of a sudden her nails dug into my chest. The force in which she grabbed hold of me shocked and scared me. Her nails penetrated my skin and started fearing the damage she could do with her psycho rage. The pain was excruciating. I turned my head and told Lamar back up. She had entrenched her nails deep into my chest. Lamar was stunned and didn't know what to do.

"Back up, Lamar!" I yelled.

Finally he put the truck in reverse. She had ripped flesh and had part of my skin and chest in her fingernails. My chest immediately started bleeding from the four very deep scratch marks. They must have been at least six inches long and blood red. My chest was on fire as blood started soaking my button down shirt. I told Lamar to just keep driving. We were getting the hell out of there, and because Betty had sabotaged my truck, she couldn't follow. I was shocked and stunned at the ferocity of her attack right in front of my daughter.

I was able to take a deep breath and finally relaxed into my seat. We started making our way to Gainesville, Georgia. It was nice to get away for the weekend. Lamar was pretty shocked after witnessing, up close, the Beast in action. I guess I had never really told Lamar about the full extent of Betty's antics. He had a basic understanding of the craziness and I was embarrassed that I was ever involved with this psychotic. I'm not really sure he had ever witnessed anything as intense as that before. We spent the weekend having a great time in Gainesville with his uncle, "Turtle," and his cousin, Scottie. They all were around the same age and had grown up like brothers. We spent the weekend drinking too much and flirting with girls. It was a welcome distraction. On this weekend, Lamar had me in the back of his truck as I had drunk too much and passed out. Instead of taking me back to his house the boys thought it would be fun to take me around in the back of his truck. I think I helped them talk with some girls, from my foggy memory. I could hear some girls saying, "Aww, poor baby; is he ok?" Lamar would say, "Yes, he is fine," all the while I am completely shit bombed. No harm no foul, and he put up with me doing that to him in Morgantown, so turnabout is fair play.

With a false sense of security, I felt relieved that Betty was on her way home with Jasmine. I had to suffer a little emotional and physical torture but at least she was heading back to Kentucky. Saying goodbye to Scottie and Turtle, Lamar and I headed back to base from our weekend. No sign of the Beast Sunday evening so I was able to relax. On Monday I got up and ate chow with Lamar. We spent our day doing some PT and cleaning our weapons. A pretty easy day considering. We had our final formation for the day and were dismissed for liberty. I started walking with Lamar to the chow hall and out of nowhere pulls up a military police vehicle. Immediately panic set in; what had Betty done? Did she tell the MP's that I had hit her or something else? I was sick to my stomach knowing they were there for me. I just knew it. The back door from the police vehicle opened and there she was! Out comes the Beast! I couldn't believe it. She walked up to me with a psychotic grin on her face knowing she had beaten me at her sick little game.

"What are you doing here?" I asked."Why didn't you go back to Kentucky?"

She just smiled and said that she went to the military police and told them that I had abandoned her and Jasmine without any money and that I had physically assaulted her. So the MP's put her and Jasmine up in the abused spouse home on base. She had truly taken things to another level. I wasn't surprised.

Pretty much using them as her own limo service, the MPs dropped her off and picked her up at whatever time she told them. She was to report to them if I became physical with her. They would immediately take me into custody. I had never touched her in the first place! This was unbelievable. A nice big report came to my commanding officer's office. I found myself standing at attention once again, explaining things to my CO. What saved my ass was my gunny sergeant remembered what happened to me over in Okinawa and had signed off on me going on emergency leave. I had told him that I didn't want to go on emergency leave, but my wife was unstable. He remembered all of this and talked to the captain for me. I was so relieved. The captain dismissed it like nothing had happened thanks to the gunny who spoke up for me.

Another close call, I thought.

However, I still had Betty to contend with. The MPs believed everything she said and I was guilty until proven innocent. She had shelter, food, and a damn police escort to take her anywhere she wanted around the base. Right around this time, I started having nightmares about her knocking on my barracks door and killing me. I couldn't sleep through the night because knowing I had to deal with her tomorrow and the next day and the next. I felt like I was suffocating. She continued to stay up my ass every day. I was in Beast prison. After a couple of weeks, after I thought it would never end, I finally caved. I told her we might give things another chance, and she needed to go home. Of course, I was lying, but she bought it. She lived in some kind of fantasyland. I just felt relieved that she was finally going back to Kentucky. I must have aged 20 years that month. I felt like I was in a Betty vice grip. What sickened me most was how she used my daughter. The Beast had no regard for Jasmine's welfare and what this might be doing to her psychologically. Her madness blinded her when it came to our daughter and I didn't know what to do about it.

The largest live-fire exercise done in the Marine Corps without actually going to war with a hostile nation is CAX, (combined arms exercise), conducted at 29 Palms in the Mojave Desert, in California. This is where you see and feel the full weight of the firepower of a Marine Corps with all air support at your disposal. We touched down landing at Camp Pendleton, the second largest Marine Corps base after Camp Lejeune, before being transported to 29 Palms. One company typically relieves another company and you live in the desert for three weeks with the scorpions, sidewinder rattlesnakes, and coyotes. During the day you spend a great deal of time firing weapons and blowing shit up.

The weapon assigned to me at this point was the SAW, squad automatic weapon, the smaller caliber version of the M60 Echo Machine Gun. It is a fully automatic weapon that has a two hundred round container of ammo attached underneath the gun.

At the time we arrived, word got out that something happened to a Marine during the previous training exercise. Not enough scuttlebutt came out for us to even take a guess. I knew something was serious once I saw people running around and a helicopter fly in with some top-level brass. Apparently, they had the final combined exercise and had left a road guard out without picking him up. When you have so many weapons firing down range it is important to block the roads that could potentially put cars and human lives in harm's way. So, road guards are deployed to the at-risk roads before any live fire exercise commences. Unfortunately, one Marine was left out in the desert when the company came in, done with their training. Since it was the end of the training, everyone was given a 36-hour leave and the Marine was left unaccounted for three and a half days before anyone even thought to look for him.

Shit hit the fan and all of us were sent out there combing the desert, searching for this missing Marine. We looked for four days straight as numerous helicopters flew overhead. Every officer and non-commissioned officer that had anything to do with leaving the Marine unaccounted for in the desert was relieved of command. Word started to get around that the Marine had made his way to Mexico and sold his M-16 to party in Tijuana. Unfortunately this is common practice in the military; rumors and misinformation come from the leadership in order to not pay or delay benefits to the surviving family members. We all knew he was dead; no way could someone make it seven days in 125 degree heat with no water or food. It was a sad and unfortunate set of circumstances. We called off the search and began our CAX training. The Marine's body was found just over a month later near a surface road.

Our first morning of live fire training had my platoon taking a flanking approach to the target down range as the rest of the company fired upon the target. My squad was on point. I was with Lamar, Jim, and Troy when all of a sudden we started taking fire from an M-60 machine gun. Rocks and sand started exploding around us as we immediately got down into the ground and hung on for dear life. I felt the ground vibrate as the 7.62-millimeter rounds hit the ground all around us. All I could feel was dirt and sand landing all over me. Each of us looked at each other in terror, as we knew it was just a matter of time before we were all dead. I couldn't believe I was going to die at the hands of my own company. With quick thinking, Jim saved us; he was carrying an M203, an M-16 with a grenade launcher. He was carrying grenade flares, quickly loaded one up in his grenade launcher and sent it into the air. Luckily that stopped the M-60 from firing on our position and we were all grateful to walk away with our lives. Needless to say we didn't finish our training exercise that day. Each and every one of us was pretty shook up but that didn't stop us from going out for training the following day.

A lot of pranks were played, given that most Marines are in the 19 to 25-year-old age range. I was the brunt of one after passing out on a cot after coming in from training. My mouth was wide open and I had been snoring for a while. Corporal Cruz spotted me sleeping, grabbed a big chunk of Skoal and proceeded to drop a large amount of it directly into my mouth. Instantly I jumped up, shocked awake, gagging and yelling. I was so pissed and sick at the same time. Puke jettisoned out of my mouth as a bunch of my friends started laughing at me. I finally regained some composure and found out who had done it to me. I went running after Cruz, but he ran to his buddy who just so happened to be a sergeant. It was the only thing that saved him from getting his ass kicked. No way was I going to let him get away unscathed so I waited for Cruz to go to chow that evening and filled his sleeping bag full of hundreds of pounds of rock and sand. I zipped it up and left it looking just like it had been on his cot. None of us went to sleep before dark, typically, so this would be a perfect payback for filling my mouth full of that shit. I let a few of my buddies in on what I had done and everyone waited for Cruz to hit the sack. I heard, "Milano, you fucking asshole!" as he discovered his sleeping bag was weighted down with rocks and sand that would take him a long time to clean out given it was so dark. I laughed my ass off with Lamar and Troy. "Hey Cruz, I thought I would give you a few extra pillows in your sleeping bag. I hope you appreciate it!" I yelled to him as he unloaded all of the shit I had dumped into his sleeping bag. Just to add a little extra payback, I did the same thing to him the next day as well.

My entire company sat along the roadway before getting ready to unleash a massive amount of lead downrange. All of the platoon commanders and platoon sergeants were checking out the targets we were getting ready to light up. We sat, sweating in the crazy heat when all of a sudden we heard our CO Captain Sullivan of 1st Battalion 2nd Marines A Company on the radio.

"Check one, Grid 734533, Direction 4805," he said over the radio.

Now, this command is only given to the mortar squad who launch explosive mortar rounds. He had called for one mortar to be fired downrange to check the distance of his coordinates.

Earlier, Captain Dickhead, as he had become known to us, told one of the lieutenants to go check on the targets we were going to engage that day. He wanted to see how effective our rounds would be at the end of the live-fire exercises for the day. For some reason, he forgot that he had told the lieutenant to do that, as well as the rest of the company leadership.

Right at that time he turned around and asked where all of the platoon commanders were. All of us pointed downrange toward the targets. "Cease Fire! Cease Fire!" he screamed into the radio but it was too late. We all heard the 'foop' sound of a mortar being fired and the whistle in the air. Captain Dickhead's eyes grew wide and we saw the fear in his face. He ran like a man possessed toward the Humvee and started it up. Rocks flew, he gunned it so hard. He drove hard and fast toward the group that had made their way downrange.

The rest of us yelled at the top of our lungs, "Get down! Get down!" The group downrange had almost reached the target. They turned around, but couldn't understand what we were saying, they were so far away. Each one of them put their hands up in the air, motioning "What are you yelling at us for?" We yelled it over and over to no avail. I had a horrible pit in my stomach as I waited for the worst-case scenario to happen and a splashdown of the mortar round in the kill zone. I just waited to see all of my senior leadership gone, blown to bits right in front of my eyes. It was one of the most horrible and scary experiences of my life.

"Kaboom!"

The mortar exploded 300 yards behind them, not close enough to do much damage besides hurting some of their eardrums a bit. I'm not sure how the captain didn't get into hot water over that major fuck up, but somehow, as with most things in the military, it was never reported.

Even Captain Dickhead, who sounded like Mickey Mouse when he spoke, was shaken up knowing he had almost killed eight people with one command into a radio. I named him from how he handled himself over the death of one of my Marine brothers and a good friend. He had given us a speech earlier in the year back in Camp Lejeune when one of my friends committed suicide after finding out about his fiancée cheating on him. My friend, Steve, put a gun to his head and pulled the trigger. Instead of being compassionate or considerate to the situation and tragedy of someone so young committing suicide, he gave a speech.

"Men, if you are thinking of committing suicide, I suggest getting in your car and driving really, really fast, then drive yourself into a wall," he casually said. "I don't want to do the paperwork on my ammo being used to kill you."

What a fucking douche bag. My buddy was in Bravo Company still and I hadn't spent as much time with him as when I was in B Company. You realize that life is so short; even with all of the torture of the Beast, that thought never came to my mind. It hurt me quite a bit that he took his own life needlessly over a woman. I didn't understand it.

We finally finished our CAX rotation and were set

loose for our 36. Every single Marine in my company was accounted for; they made damn sure that mistake was not going to be repeated. Lamar, Dale and I snuck off the base and found the most shithole dive bar I'd ever seen in the local town. At the end of the bar was a barfly named Maggie. Of course, the three of us go take up seats next to her and start chatting her up. You could tell right away she was going to be down with any suggestion that we made. She actually was semi attractive, but a bit worn out. Maggie asked, "Do you boys want to come over to my place?" As horny as we all were, we said "yes" simultaneously and off to Maggie's we went. She went into her bedroom to get something more comfortable on as we passed out the condoms we had just picked up at the convenience store. Fortunately or unfortunately, I lost rock, paper, scissor and was to go last. Lamar was first up to bat. Maggie was definitely a naughty girl and left her bedroom door open so we could see Lamar ramming her. Dale was growing frustrated because Lamar was taking too long. He made his way into her bedroom, placed his hand on Lamar's ass and pushed it down in conjunction with Lamar's fucking moments. "Hurry up, hurry up," he repeated while doing this. I almost pissed my pants it was so funny to see. Lamar turned around, "Get your fucking hand off me, asshole!" Of course Lamar lost his hard on and was never going to get it up after Dale had put his hands on his ass! Sick fuck Dale went right in and commenced to fuck Maggie hard and fast. Within a minute fast. I was still laughing at Lamar as he was out in the living room bitching to me about Dale. I told him to go in there and do the same thing. He said, "No way am I touching that dude's ass, he is a sick bastard." All my desire to fuck Maggie had gone away, so as soon as Dale came out we got out of there.

We finally got on the plane back to Camp Lejeune. Betty had left me alone because the Marine Corps wouldn't tell her exact, specific details about my training exercises. It was so nice that she didn't know when I would be coming or going.

As we turned our weapons into the armory and made our way to the barracks I was happy it is was Friday and we would get the weekend to recuperate. I'm just chilling in my room waiting for end of day formation and Santiago comes into my room. Santiago was married and lived off base. We had been assigned desert camouflage for our desert training in the Mojave Desert. He says "Hey Milano can I leave my camos here for the weekend?" Knowing that these are "cool" and a lot of Marines like the idea of having a pair of them I said "that's not a good idea, I'm gonna be gone all weekend and I don't want to be responsible for them." Santiago was from New York and was Puerto Rican and definitely had a New York attitude to him. Our platoon Sgt couldn't stand him as he was Puerto Rican too, but Santiago would always wear 20+ gold necklaces and some ridiculous kangaroo hat whenever he wasn't in uniform. It drove Staff Sgt Reyes crazy.

Santiago was relentless. "Aww come on man, nothing is going to happen to them, I don't want to bring them home."

"Hey if you want to leave them that's fine, just know I'm not taking responsibility for them, I'm serious," I said.

The weekend goes by and Monday I get up at the butt crack of dawn, as usual. Lamar and I make our way to chow and come back to our rooms. A few minutes later Santiago comes into my room and asks "where are my camos?" I hadn't paid attention or noticed that they were gone. "I have no idea," I said. He starts raising his voice to me and starts cussing me. This isn't sitting well with me so I said "I have no idea where the fuck your camos are, I told not to leave them and I wasn't responsible!" I left my room before I blew my top, as he was a hot head.

I walk into Lamar's room right next door to mine and try to calm down. Santiago burst into the room and started yelling at me in front of Lamar and Jim. I snapped and threw him onto Lamar's rack and started raining punches down on him. I hadn't put my boots on yet so I was slipping as I was holding him down and punching him furiously. Blood started splattering all over the wall and some onto Lamar's sheets. Lamar and Jim just watched and let me give him a beating, they knew he deserved it so they let it happen. I hit him enough to where he said, "stop, stop, I'm sorry, enough." I stopped and turned around and left the room. I didn't realize the damage I had done to his face until later in the day.

At morning formation Santiago wasn't present as he had to go to sickbay and get stitched up. The rest of the platoon heard what happened, but no one said a word. As we came to attention Staff Sgt Reyes walked up to me. Oh shit is all I could think. He reached out his hand to shake mine.

"Good job Milano, don't worry about Santiago, I've got you covered."

I cracked a huge smile. Santiago didn't talk to me for a few weeks, but eventually, we made peace with each other. Just like brothers that fight, you are still brothers.

I got a crazy idea one day that I should become a brown bagger and live off base. The only problem with that is that you have to have a wife living with you. My platoon commander and platoon sergeant knew I was married, so it was as simple as saying, "Sir, my wife is moving with me off base; do I need to give up my room?" And just like that, I was able to go and look for a place to live off the base. I was the one married guy that really wasn't married.

We looked around and I found a trailer park that had a few trailers for rent. I decided that we needed a party house and from that day on, we had a place to party.

I set myself up with a sweet ass trailer in a rundown trailer park. My buddies loved the idea. There were girls around all the time and I got knocks at my door at all hours of the night. My buddies would show up with random girls and until that point had no place to fuck them unless they wanted to pay for a hotel room. A lot of drinking and fucking went on in that trailer. I can imagine what it would be like in a frat house because my trailer felt like one. There was a woman that lived in a trailer four spots down from mine that gave head to at least four of my buddies. The day finally came when we had to give up Casa De Milano because we were being deployed to Hampton Beach, Virginia for two months. It was a sad day for all of us, but it was a nice run.

Training operations in Virginia were pretty intensive and involved other branches of the military. We were transported on an a landing platform for helicopters, just like the ship we spent time on in the Mediterranean. It picked us up from Cherry Point and after a short trip to Virginia, we boarded helicopters and landed in an LZ to start our training operations. We were going up against the 92nd Airborne. They had set up a defensive position and our mission was to defeat them by launching attacks from helicopters and Amtraks (Amphibious Landing Vehicles. The first part of the raid lasted four days.

We moved through the woods tactically and

deliberately, not knowing exactly where the Rangers were dug in. On the last night before we found their location and planned our attack we came across a river we needed to cross. This was a challenge, getting over a hundred Marines over a pretty heavy flowing body of water without being detected by the enemy. Luckily our advanced scouts came across a downed tree lying across the entire river. It was large enough to support a number of people at one time walking across it. "We need the WSQ up here right away!" I heard and of course, was like, "Shit." Since I was the Company's WSQ, water survival qualified swimmer, I knew what that meant. I was tasked with jumping into the river in case anyone fell in. The unfortunate part was that it was December and in the thirties. As I made my way up toward the front of the tactical formation my buddies gave me shit, telling me they hoped someone would fall in so I would freeze my ass off jumping in after them. All I could think to do was strip down my camos and stand there as naked as the day I was born. I had quit wearing underwear quite a while ago due to the nastiness of having underwear on for weeks at a time in the field. It was quite a funny scene as each Marine in my company went by and saw me standing naked. I heard a lot of shrinkage jokes as each one passed by, but the most shit I received was from my own platoon. They really enjoyed seeing me there, all exposed to the weather and everything else.

Finally, each guy made it across and I put my clothes back on and joined my platoon. We set up to attack the guys from the 92nd Airborne and executed at 0300. By and large, the raid was successful and we got to kick back a bit afterwards. It had been almost a week since we had any hot food and it was nice to get some hot chow. The only problem was that we began to hear rumors that one of our fellow Marines hadn't checked in with his radio. He was part of Force Recon and had parachuted in a few days earlier. None of the commanders had heard from him. Within a few hours we knew something was up because we hadn't begun any additional training exercises; we were just sitting at our base camp. Word finally came that we were going to go on a search for the missing Marine. This was the second time in my military career that I went looking for a lost Marine brother and I remembered what happened to the Marine in 29 Palms.

We started making our way through the woods in a spread out formation, each one of us looked hard, hoping we would find him and that he would be alive. Suddenly, as if we all seemed to look up at the same time, there he was, up in a tree about 40 feet above our heads. His body was mangled and his rifle snapped, hanging from his torso. Eyes were black from filling with blood due to the severe impact of hitting the tree at such a high velocity. His chute hadn't opened and for some reason, he hadn't been able to deploy his backup. It was a sick sight to see and each one of us was affected differently. It started to hit home how dangerous being in the Marine Corps could be, even during peacetime. We waited for the commander to get to our location and then a few of his guys from his unit climbed the tree to bring him down. Very surreal situation. We suspended the rest of the training operation and made our way back to Camp Lejeune a bit early.

Luckily during this period, I didn't hear from the Beast too much. The one nice thing about being out for training exercises was that even with her over the top skills in finding where I was, she could never find me when I was out training.

Chapter 21

Every once in a while we got a fresh batch of Marines that had just finished boot camp and School of Infantry. Every time, reporting to the fleet, they showed up wide-eyed and scared, not knowing what was in store for them. Sgt Reeves was in full control of the platoon as the acting platoon sergeant. He called for me to come down. "Milano, come down here!" I had been in the Marine Corps just over three years at this point and knew how things worked. I was very clean cut, with boyish looks. Somewhat a picture perfect Marine. The exact profile of a Marine officer. Reeves handed me two Lieutenant Bars and told me to fuck with the new guys.

We had a few guys standing watch, as this was a big no-no, impersonating an officer, even if for fun. Sgt Reeves instructed the new Marines to get ready for an inspection from the 'Platoon Commander. The entire platoon lined up in front of their rooms, standing at attention. The three new Marines had their duffle bags full of the gear you receive when you arrive at boot camp at their sides. I walked up to Sgt Reeves and barked out, "Sgt Reeves, are your men ready for inspection?" He snapped to attention, "Yes, Sir!"

I was pretty impressed everyone was holding it together and not laughing in front of the new guys. I continued to berate Sgt Reeves and I have to admit, was having a blast with it. I moved on to each Marine in the platoon, commenting on each one, finding something wrong with them. "Cpl Lee, your fucking boots look like shit, did you take a shit and wipe them down with it? When is the last time you shined them, you fucking asshole?" By the time I reached the new guys, who had been strategically placed at the end of the line, they were shitting their pants.

"What's your name, Marine?" I saw the fear and terror in his eyes. "PFC Jones, Sir!" he called out. I looked him up and down and told him, "You look like a bag of shit!" I could hear some of the guys starting to crack up a bit behind me. I spun around quickly and yelled, "Lock it up, Marines!" I told all of the newbies to dump their gear; we were going to make sure they had everything. You could hear all of their shit hitting the deck in front of them as I continued yelling at them for no reason whatsoever.

"Get down and give me fifty!"

They hit the deck and started pumping out push-ups as fast as they could. It was getting harder and harder for everyone trying to hold it together and not bust out laughing as I fucked with the new guys. At that point, I told each of them to get their e-tool and go dig me a foxhole. I pointed to a sandy area down in front of the barracks. "Do it now!" They flew down the stairs with their e-tools in their hands. Furiously they started digging, trying to please their new platoon commander.

I went back to my room and changed out my Lieutenant bars for Corporal ones. We all leaned on the rails and watched the newbies dig their foxholes. We were finally able to laugh and enjoy the hazing to the full extent. After an hour Sgt Reeves yelled down to them and told them to get back upstairs and stow away their gear sitting in front of their rooms. It was getting close to formation time where we would really get in front of the platoon commander. I waited in my room and stayed out of sight until the last minute so I would be the last one coming into formation. The guys saved me a spot right next to the new guys. I came up behind them and took my spot right next to them.

"How are you doing, Marines?" I said in the nicest voice possible.

The looks on their faces were priceless, as they looked right at my corporal pendants, seeing I wasn't an officer. Everyone busted out laughing as our prank reached its conclusion. The new guys weren't even that upset about it and laughed about it right after formation. Of course, I apologized, but it was all in good fun with no harm done. The real platoon commander was a real sweetheart compared to the guy they thought was leading them.

That didn't stop other guys from messing with them as every new guy goes through a certain amount of abuse when they join the platoon. They were sent to go get a silencer for the M-60 from the armory and to get the call signs for the day from the lieutenant. None of these things existed of course, but it was fun to tell a new guy to go ask for it. The Marine running the armory would always go along with the gag and give the Marine some completely irrelevant item that needed to be thrown out anyway.

The best part was telling the new guy to put it to use or set it up, whatever the item was. This usually went on for a while until they had been with us for a bit and then we would get more new guys to fuck with. At that time, they would get to enjoy being part of the prank.

One of the sick and twisted games you play in the Marine Corps that sharpen your aggressiveness and killer instinct was a game called 'killer ball." Usually, you would face off against another platoon from another company. The game was really simple in nature. It was a large, blown up rubber ball that was 10 feet high. The object of the game was to get the ball to the other side of the field and through the soccer goal. Rules? That was the kicker, there were no rules. Usually, there would be an extra day off on the line for the winner.

The platoon sergeant blew the whistle as we squared off against our fellow Marines. Our big guys started pushing the ball. A few other guys and I ran around the side of the ball, jumped through the air and started hitting the other platoon with flying elbows. We tried to not hit them in the face, but sometimes it was unavoidable. It was mostly controlled fighting with an objective of getting a large ball down the field. This was a game right up many of the guys' alley as they thoroughly enjoyed laying people out. I stayed close to Lamar as we effectively started taking people out.

We were absolutely exhausted by the time we got the ball down the field and finally into the soccer goal. Mercifully they blew the whistle and the game ended at 1-0. The platoon sergeants put this game together every few months just to keep us in check. In the Marines, you train to kill your enemy so this kind of activity made sense if you think about it.

Chapter 22

I was a short timer by this point. In other words, I didn't have too much longer in the Marine Corps. I started to see my friends get out and knew I didn't have much longer myself. Lamar got out a few months before I did and things just didn't feel the same. The last deployment I was scheduled to go on was cold weather training. By far the most dreaded training in the Marine Corps. We went to Northern California first. I had grown up cross-country skiing in Massachusetts and was pretty good at it.

Part of the training was being evaluated on your skiing skills. I was one of the better skiers in the group so I became a designated scout skier. Our job was to recon ahead of the unit and find the best routes to take. I got in the best shape from skiing constantly for three weeks straight. The nice thing about being a scout skier was that we skied almost the whole time in California. Each day we would get up, fix chow and go find the best path for the rest of the company to take. After spending three weeks in the mountains we finally finished that part of cold weather training. As a scout skier, I was allowed to ski down the mountain while everyone else had to hump down it. It was just under 10 miles to reach the bottom and it was such a rush.

At the end of the day, my buddies returned from hiking down the mountain. It felt like heaven sitting in heated tents versus the cold conditions we had been exposed to for the past three weeks. We were able to get some chow and sleep in a large, heated tent that night before leaving for the second phase of cold weather training in Wisconsin.

The rest of the company got ready and we flew to Wisconsin to complete the next phase of our cold weather training. Who the hell lives in Wisconsin? Are these people on crack? It was constantly cold there. It didn't even warm up during the day. We spent the next month outside in the cold, eating MREs (meals ready to eat) and just trying to survive the freezing temperatures. We were training to fight the Russians on their home soil. They were still the enemy at this point. I knew more useless information about their tanks, helicopters, and weapons than I knew what to do with.

The conditions in Wisconsin were absolutely brutal. Bone-chilling cold that absolutely hurts you to the core. The first night that we slept out in the cold we got the wake-up call at five a.m. It is really hard to move fast and get dressed in -20 degrees below temperatures. My new platoon sergeant absolutely refused to get out of his sleeping bag. He had been in the Marine Corps for over twelve years and was what we call a lifer, someone who planned on staying in the military until they retired. The problem he had was that he had been in an Amtrak Company pretty much his entire career and was not used to harsh conditions. Whenever he was out in the field, previous to joining us, he would just order the Amtrak driver to turn on the engine and warm the interior of the vehicle. He had never been exposed to these kinds of conditions and just wasn't mentally or physically prepared to deal with it.

Staff Sgt Roberts just couldn't get out of his bag; he didn't have the will to do so. Captain Dickhead stood over top of him yelling, "Sgt Roberts, get out of that bag now and get your men ready to move!" Roberts simply replied, "No," and that was it. This company commander was the worst one we had ever had and he made an example out of this enlisted guy.

The sleeping bags were so absolutely warm and comfortable no matter what the temperature was. Those sleeping bags were amazing and the engineers who designed them did an amazing job. We slept right on top of the snow but stayed warm. We had to bring everything into our bags with us at night or it would be destroyed. Our weapons, canteens, boots, clothes, food, everything. Otherwise, it would freeze solid. Sgt Roberts had just ruined 12 years of service in the Marine Corps because of the conditions we were put through in our training. He would have stayed in for another eight years and been able to draw a pension the rest of his life but that one decision blew it for him. You have to be tough-minded to get through some of the shit they throw at you.

I didn't get to see what happened with Sgt Roberts, but we never saw him again. We heard a while later he was discharged. Not sure if it was honorable or a general discharge, but I felt bad for him. I had given four years of my life and that was hard enough, never mind twelve.

In some karmic justice, Captain Dickhead decided to show everyone what it was like to be trapped in an avalanche. We dug an eight-foot hole for him to get into and we used long sticks, to try and locate him, so we would know how to find someone in an avalanche situation. He climbed into the hole and was covered up with snow. I thought it was crazy, but he was mister badass. He spent about fifteen minutes covered with eight feet of snow on top of him. Within an hour, he came down with pneumonia and had to be medevaced down to the camp. It was awesome to see him in distress like he was, especially since he had been so cold about my buddy committing suicide. I hated him and was glad he got a little bit of karmic justice to come bite him in the ass. After all of the cross-country skiing, building snow shelters and training for 30 days in the coldest conditions imaginable, we finally got the word that cold weather training was over and headed to the base.

The entire company received some much-needed liberty after we got to the base in Wisconsin. Everybody was absolutely frazzled. Besides boot camp, cold weather training is definitely the hardest thing to go through in the Marine Corps. Most of the guys hung around the barracks and took showers. It had been a solid two months since anybody had a shower or slept on a mattress. It was nice to finally feel warm again.

Some other people from our company went out to the enlisted club to have a few drinks and blow off some steam. I stayed at the barracks and just chilled out knowing I would be getting out of the Marine Corps days after we returned to Camp Lejeune. It was somewhat surreal with everything that I had been through with the Beast and the military, but I was ready to start my new adventure. I did a lot of self-reflecting.

No one really knew what happened, but we got word that one of our sergeants got jumped on the way back from the club by some of the Marine reservists. Sgt Reeves, our new platoon sergeant, came into the barracks, told everyone what happened and said, "Let's go get them mother fuckers!" Almost the entire company followed him out the door.

This all happened right around midnight. Sgt Reeves walked out the door, followed by at least 100 marines behind him, and headed toward the reserve barracks. There was a fire watch on patrol at the reserve barracks.

You could see his eyes get large and fill with fear as he saw the mob heading his way. In a panic, he tried to hold the door shut on the mob of angry Marines. The door was subsequently smashed down and A Company rolled through the reserve barracks like a pure, destructive, battering ram. They began pulling every reservist out of their racks from a dead sleep and started pummeling them. No mercy; the reservists were getting hit really hard and most of them had no idea what the hell was going on. They rolled around in pain and agony from the beat down they were taking.

I imagine it was the built up rage from being in the cold for two straight months. It has to do something to your psyche to be in those kinds of conditions for so long. The destructive force of this group of guys was amazing to watch. I stayed on the sideline, just watching since I was due to get out of the Marine Corps two days after we got back form cold weather training. I wasn't going to do anything to mess that up.

The Marine mob rolled from one barrack to another just pounding all of these poor reservists. You can't tell who is an officer and who is an enlisted person because none of them had uniforms on. They did the same thing with one barrack, and it just so happened that these guys were all officers. The scene was absolute pandemonium, like something you might see in a movie. By the time it was over, the mob had gone through five barracks, beat the hell out of at least a hundred guys, and all of the fighting moved outside as you saw Marine versus Marine going at each other. I had moved outside to see all of the action and was standing right next to the gunny sergeant; we commented on how out of control all of this was. He just shook his head as no one could stop what was going on until it ran its course.

Shit hit the fan after all of the punches were finally thrown. We had a formation at 2:30 a.m. The company commander, finally recovering from pneumonia, told everyone that there were going to be court marshals for everyone involved. All of the officers that were beat up came by our formation. One by one, they got in front of everyone and asked to see our hands to see if they had marks on them from hitting. They also took a good long look at everyone's face to try and see if they recognized anybody.

One of the reserve officers said, "This Marine hit me and I want him charged!" They actually pulled out one of my guys, who happened to be in my squad and was standing right next to me. He was a large, muscle-bound black guy with a massive mole on his cheek. He was one of the softest spoken and non-confrontational people in the platoon. I personally saw him stay in his rack when I went out following the mob. He was there when I returned, so I know he had absolutely nothing to do with the chaos that had transpired that early morning.

This officer was pissed that he had a black eye and wanted to blame it on somebody, but I was not going to let someone burn for something he didn't do. I stepped forward and said, "That Marine stayed in his rack and had nothing to do with this mess and if they bring charges, I would testify on his behalf." I knew for a fact that he stayed in his rack the whole time.

Before we went out to formation, Sgt Reeves yelled out, "No ring leaders! No ring leaders!" and we knew exactly what he meant. They would be looking for someone to make an example out of, and as long as no one talked, they couldn't pin it on anyone. You always have your fellow Marine's back, even when they are wrong, so none of us talked. The gunny sent him back to Camp Lejeune a couple days early to take some of the pressure off and allow things to cool down. These officers were all reservists and would have to take time off from their real jobs to attend any court marshals. All I could think of was having to delay getting out because I would be a witness to a hundred court marshals. Not that they would get anything out of me anyway.

This eventually all blew over and we returned to Camp Lejeune. They wanted to go after Sgt. Reeves, but couldn't find anybody to say that he was the ringleader. So his charges were dropped as well. Two days after we got back to Camp Lejeune, I was discharged from the Marine Corps.

My last day was pretty interesting because one of my buddies, Porter, who used to come into my room singing 'kill the white man' when he woke me up every day, decided to pull a prank on me and throw a huge amount of toilet paper into my truck since he knew I was leaving. I ran after him, but finally gave up and cleaned out my car, delayed only a little bit. I couldn't believe that after four years of giving blood, sweat, and tears to the Marines, Porter delayed me in leaving the base and starting my life as a civilian once again.

After getting my truck cleaned up, I began my journey. Each morning the MPs put orange cones up to change traffic to a three-lane road coming into the base while one lane went out. It was the reverse in the afternoons. Getting to the middle of the base took a while, as it is five to six miles after entering the front gates. I saw an opportunity and became very rebellious on my way off the base. Seeing all of the orange cones that I had driven by so many times as I'd left base made me see red for some reason. I decided to drive over each and every cone for a five-mile stretch as I left the base. I honked at the MP and said, "I'm fucking out of here!" as I finally left. My truck had cones stuck underneath the under panel for a few more miles as I made my way through Jacksonville.

Chapter 23

It had been relatively quiet for a while on the Beast front over the past year so I actually had some hope that she would be relatively reasonable to deal with once I got out.

I began my drive to Lexington, Kentucky to start the next chapter of my life. I loved my buddies and my time in the Marine Corps, but definitely wanted more out of life and couldn't believe that people stay in the Marines for 20 or 30 years. Every person I knew that stayed in for a 20 year stretch looked like they were in their 60's when they were only 38 to 45. It is a hard life, being in the Marines like that.

I figured I could get a job, go to school and spend time being a father to my daughter. Because of all the shit Betty had put me through I hadn't spent much time around Jasmine while I was in the Marine Corps because I had to contend with her. I just couldn't do it. I didn't know how Betty would act if I lived that close to her, but I thought I would give it a try for Jasmine's sake. I stayed in a hotel for a week while I looked for an apartment. I saw an ad in the paper looking for security work that paid $1,000 dollars a week. The ad encouraged all former military to please apply. So I did. I went into the interview still looking like a Marine except I wore a nice suit. This guy hired me on the spot. I had been discharged from the Marines for nine days when I landed this job.

The actual job was in New York City. He wanted me to be a supervisor because of my military experience. I was 22 and pretty stoked to have a great paying job. I only made $16,000 dollars my last year in the Marine Corps. I couldn't believe I had landed a job paying this much money. Once I arrived in New York, I soon found out why it paid so much.

The New York Daily News, with a circulation of two million papers a day, had a labor dispute, and the drivers and machine press operators were getting ready to go on strike. Senior management decided to hire scabs to take over to keep the paper running. What they needed me, and the other 200 guards they had hired, to do was protect the company property and not allow the striking workers to do any damage. One of the tasks they needed us to do was follow the delivery trucks around to make sure they weren't sabotaged.

The company had flown in 200 guards from all over the country and stationed us right across the river from New York. When I first arrived, the boss, "Mr. E," pulled me aside. I was wearing a suit while everyone else wore casual attire. He wanted me to work with him in the 'command post.' Of course, I said sure. My job was to coordinate the drivers and the shift changes to get the guards to their posts. I was also responsible for paying the $50,000 dollar hotel bill each week and picking up the per diem money for all of the guards.

This was always quite an interesting endeavor. I always met with this guy named Dave at some designated location like a bus station, train station, or diner, who would sign for $100,000 dollars of cash, and he would hand me a briefcase full of money. For a while, I started having thoughts that I was working for the mob. To be honest, I probably was. Mr. E had a real bad drug problem and the way we communicated with the guards on their posts was by utilizing Motorola walkie-talkies. Mr. E got on the walkie-talkie after snorting a number of lines of coke and for some reason, didn't think our client, the New York Daily News, was monitoring our dialogue using their equipment. This was a big mistake for Mr. E. He had delegated pretty much all of his responsibilities to me and I was running the entire operation within a month of starting the position.

I started noticing that guards who had been fired still had paychecks coming into the office. At first I didn't think too much about it, but started to realize Mr. E was cashing these checks from guards that were no longer working. The number was growing pretty large, too, up to 12 guards that had been let go were still getting checks and we kept billing the NY Daily News like they had been working their 84 hours. I said something to Mr. E and he quickly shut me down, telling me to leave it alone. I knew they had some shady shit going down. The Motorola incident finally got Mr. E fired and I was the only person who knew how to run things, so I took over the entire operation. It wasn't much different from what I was already doing, anyway.

They paid these guards eight dollars per hour and charged the New York Daily News sixteen dollars per hour for each guard. The guards worked 84 hours a week and after three months, were given a week off. I worked more like 110 hours a week. They paid me $12 dollars an hour, and of course most of my money was made working all of those hours overtime. I thought I was rich. I received $25 dollars per day in per diem money as well. I worked so much that I didn't have time to spend any money, so I started to get creative with my time.

After accumulating quite a little bit of money, I called Betty's mom and told her I'd like to send money to her for Jasmine. I didn't trust Betty as far as I could throw her. I decided to open up a joint checking account with Betty's mom in Kentucky. I did this so she could get anything for

Jasmine that she needed. I would send money to this account periodically to keep it full of money for my daughter. Betty's mom was very sweet and I truly trusted her, nothing like her daughter. It was hard to imagine that someone so evil came from her.

After getting all of the processes down and the shift changes perfected, I started to be able to work less than 100 each week. My day was pretty much the same; I got up early and made sure the day shift took over for the night shift. I had a crew of drivers that delivered the guards to the sites and a few special guards that did surveillance on the delivery trucks. They followed the trucks with rental cars. One day I was sitting in the command center and two large Italian gentlemen came into the room. They introduced themselves, "Hi, I am Antonio and this is my brother, Franco." These were the DiMarco brothers and they told me that the owners of the company had asked them to come help me out in the command post. They were both from Paterson, New Jersey and had known the owners of the security company for 20 years. They were strictly there just to observe and assist as needed. Both brothers had the typical Italian mob build. They stood about 5'8" or so and had massive guts that they carried around like they were pregnant. They didn't walk, exactly, but waddled in a slow, methodical manner. Both sported large gold chains, ridiculous bling-bling Rolex watches and very powerful cologne at all times. Each time they entered the room the smell cut through the air and I knew they were there before ever seeing them.

I wasn't stupid and knew exactly why they were there; they were making sure that the checks kept flowing for the guards that had gone home. For being mobsters they were pretty sweet guys. The owners of the company had a big scam going on and I wasn't going to rock the boat. I got to see the DiMarco brothers' checks and they made substantially more money than I did. Instead of asking questions I decided to just roll with it, keep my mouth shut and enjoy my new life.

Like any responsible twenty two year old with six times the money he previously had, I started renting limos and partying like a rock star as a way of entertaining myself and enjoying my new career. I had a complete blast in New York and took full advantage of my freedom from the Marine Corps and from Betty. I was young, free and making good money. Working twelve to fourteen hour days, I started to really get to know all of the managers at the hotel. It had a nice restaurant and a very attractive hostess that I flirted with on a regular basis named Maria. She was beautiful with cocoa skin that was so soft like a baby's bottom. She was originally from the Dominican Republic and loved to go salsa dancing.

After a while I finally got the courage to ask her out and she said that she would love to. We became close fairly fast and had a connection right from the go. I hadn't gotten involved with anyone seriously since Dana. Maria was feisty. We spent a lot of time exploring New York City. She cooked Spanish food, which I soon found out was nothing like Mexican food. It is very bland in nature, without much spice. Her favorite was plantains, fried bananas. Because I liked her so much I tried to get used to eating them, but just couldn't.

Betty called and harassed me a lot in New York. Big surprise. She said that I had broken my word by not coming back to Kentucky to help her with Jasmine. I knew it had nothing to do with Jasmine. She wanted me there so she could try to get back together with me. I was smart enough to know this by now.

Maria got to see how much Betty harassed me and did things to get under Betty's skin. When Betty called one time, wanting to talk as usual, I tried to get her off the phone, but she pulled one of her 'we need to talk' deals on me while Maria lied next to me on the bed. Maria got tired of me talking to Betty, trying to appease her, and grabbed the phone out of my hands. Instantly, I started to panic.

Maria immediately called her a fat ass bitch and told her to stop calling me so much. "Mark doesn't need to have to hear from your stupid bitch ass mouth all the damn time!" Betty lost it and had a full-on meltdown on the phone with Maria. They started fighting over the phone and finally, Maria hung up on her. She laughed and smiled at me. Maria truly believed that Betty would stop calling so much now that I had a full-time girlfriend who wasn't afraid of my soon to be ex-wife. She obviously didn't know Betty.

This just made her start calling all the time. Maria always picked up the phone and told Betty that she was about to give me head, could she call back later. Talk about stirring up a hornet's nest. However, it was pretty funny to see somebody getting the better of Betty for once. I loved it. I had a great time with Maria and my job for the next 10 months. This was a strike situation and finally both sides came to an agreement. TopSec Security wanted to keep me in New York, but I decided it would be a good time to go back to Kentucky and go to school. Betty finally made me feel guilty about not seeing Jasmine regularly. Going to school had been the plan all along when I joined the Marine Corps. I would go to college and start a career. Maria wanted to come with me to Lexington, but I wasn't ready for that just yet. I also knew what kind of shit awaited me when I returned to Kentucky from the Beast. I didn't want Maria to have to deal with any of that. She didn't know what Betty was capable of.

I said my goodbyes to Maria and promised we would stay in touch. I left New York and headed back to Kentucky. At that time, I looked up Rob. I hadn't seen him since we graduated from ITS in the early days in the Marine Corps. He had been stationed at Guantanamo Bay, Cuba. We were both happy to see each other and decided to become roommates. We looked around together and found an apartment that was fairly cheap. Our good friend, Jenna, from high school, came over and helped us fix our place up. She gave it that woman's touch. I found out later that Betty had found out that Jenna came over to see me. Betty called her and confronted her about being around Rob and I. Betty told Jenna not to come around me anymore.

Betty had every intention of getting back together with me and didn't want anybody standing in her way. My friend Jenna was a definite threat to her. Jenna didn't even tell me anything about this until a month or so later. She hadn't called me or kept in touch and I didn't know why. When I found out that Betty had tried to keep my friend away from me I became infuriated. I was so sick and tired of her trying to control my life. I called her and she denied that she had called Jenna. Such a fucking liar.

Betty began stalking me relentlessly when I moved back to Kentucky. I got a call from my sister, Gina, who needed to move in with me. She was having trouble staying with my stepmother since she graduated from high school in California. They weren't getting along so well so she wanted to come stay with me. I had an extra room for her to stay in and was happy to have my sister back in my life. So it was Gina, Rob and I living in one apartment. This didn't stop Betty from showing up all the time. She started to get her full-court press on, becoming relentless in her pursuit. She just wouldn't leave me alone, and this started to cause problems at my apartment.

One day we were out in the parking lot of my apartment, arguing as usual. The Beast was really agitated that day; she was going to have her say and I was going to listen. Her mind was so warped by that time, she always acted irrationally. Eventually I made my way past her, trying my best to just ignore her and go about my business. I was able to get into my car and start it. Her eyes were intense with rage as she wasn't able to finish her conversation.

I backed up and started to leave the parking lot when I saw the large body flying toward my windshield. A large thud; the car rocked a bit. She encompassed the entire windshield, grabbing on to the side mirror. Seeing the anger and fury in her eyes I became really scared as to what the hell she would do next. I stopped the car and she refused to get off the hood. It was astonishing, the lengths she would go to in order to try and control me. Patiently, I sat there in my car and tried to wait her out, but there was no waiting out the Beast when she was raging.

As I sat there, I wondered how many times this psycho had affected my life on a daily basis. I started to experience signs of PTSD, from dealing with Betty for so long now. My pulse always raced and heart jumped whenever I heard a phone ring or a door knock.

I started to talk to her as she laid across my hood, telling her I had to leave and she had to stop doing this. "What is wrong with you, Betty?" It was amazing how she could justify everything that she did, in her own mind. Unfortunately, because she was effective in utilizing this technique as a way to stop me from leaving or driving off, she incorporated it numerous times for the next few years. I would have thought she would be embarrassed laying on top of a car like that, but it didn't seem to bother her.

She, of course, blamed me for making her act that way. It was my fault that she did the things that she did. "You should take responsibility for making me this way!" was one of her favorite quotes.

Rob and Gina got sick of the drama show.

Betty's mother and I still had a joint account together. I thought it was a good idea to let her determine when Jasmine needed something and she would have the money to get it. I thought of this account as a cushion account for myself, too. Betty absolutely hated this, but I told her mom that I didn't trust Betty, and she knew what Betty had done with their phone bill before while I was in Okinawa, so she agreed to work with me. Lawrenceburg is a small town with only two banks in it.

Betty stole the checks out of her mother's room from our joint account and cashed a $500 dollar check at the window of the bank. The teller didn't ask her for her ID or check to see whose name was really on the account, and gave her the money. I saw the statement, was shocked to found out about this, and called the bank. The bank went into a panic, knowing they had screwed up big time. Instead of taking care of the problem, this teller went to Betty's parents' house after work with the check and begged her mom to sign it, otherwise, she would lose her job. Her mom was a very nice woman and didn't want to see this woman get fired for some conniving that Betty had done, so she signed it. I was out $500 dollars. I never forgave that bank and got revenge on them later on. I immediately closed the account so Betty couldn't pull something like that again. It pissed me off to no end that she could keep fucking me over the way she did.

I kept my word and stayed in touch with Maria from New York. She said that she wanted to come down and see me. I didn't see any reason not to have her come down so I made arrangements to get her a plane ticket to Lexington. I made it very clear to Betty to stop coming around, but of course she didn't listen to me. I knew this would be an issue when Maria came down for the weekend. I thought it would be safer if I got a room for the weekend. As the time started getting closer I began feeling the pressure. Betty could tell something was up and was relentless in her pursuit to find out what was going on. I finally just told her that Maria was coming to town and that I was spending the weekend with her. She flat out told me, "No, you're not!" She had the audacity to try and tell me what I was going to do. I was really starting to regret coming back to Kentucky. I knew it would be like this. but wanted to try and be a good dad.

I picked Maria up from the airport and we immediately went to the hotel room. I was so happy to see her. I didn't have the nerve to ask anybody out or try to date in Lexington, knowing they would have to face the wrath of the Beast. I knew she would scare the hell out of anybody that I tried to date. So, I had gone without for a couple of months. Betty did offer a few times. I would have rather stuck my dick in acid than touch her again. It creeped me out, just her offering.

So, Maria and I were really happy to see each other, to say the least. I took Maria over to my apartment later to show her where I lived. Low and behold, the Beast had begun stalking my place in anticipation of Maria coming for a visit. It gave me an instant pit in my stomach, not knowing what the fuck Beast was going to do. Betty flipped out, ran over to my car and confronted Maria. "Oh my god, Mark, she is a nigger!" I had never heard Betty use such a racist word since I'd known her. Of all the crazy things she had done, this one really shocked me. I didn't know she had racial prejudices. Maria wasn't black, white, or Dominican; she was just Maria to me.

They locked horns in the middle of the parking lot. Both had death grip holds on each other's hair as they were interlocked in a hate dance. The next thing I knew they were rolling around on the ground. I couldn't get them apart and didn't know what to do. I was worried that Betty would hurt Maria; she was bigger than her and a lot crazier. Finally, I got them separated and Maria started saying some smart-ass stuff to the Beast. Betty's eyes were filled with absolute rage and hate. It was pretty scary and I was really nervous as to what might be in store for me.

I didn't go back to my apartment for the rest of the weekend. Maria started talking about missing me and wanting to come down to Kentucky and live with me. After the episode in the parking lot, I knew it would be crazy if she moved down to Kentucky with me. I worried about Maria's safety. I feared that I might end up dead if I didn't play my cards right. It's a terrible thing to live in fear. She truly had me terrified.

She was waiting for me when I returned home from dropping Maria off at the airport. She had a crazy look in her eye that truly scared me. I tried to get into my apartment without getting into a confrontation with her, but I lived on the third floor. There was no avoiding her. I tried to physically go around her and she just kept getting in my way. I finally made it to the door and she forced her way into my house.

"Get the fuck out of my place!" I screamed.

She wanted to tell me how mad she was about Maria. I didn't want to hear it, so I tried to go over to the phone and call the police to have her removed from my apartment. As soon as I called the police, she ripped the phone out of the wall. She immediately went over to my TV and smashed it on the living room floor. She had psychotic strength, so she then picked the TV up and launched it off the balcony. It flew through the air until it finally hit the ground and exploded into a number of pieces. Immediately, I grabbed her and tried to push her out of my apartment. I got her near the door and she initiated a strategy that she used in the past and would utilize a number of times from that point on.

Betty dropped to the floor and rolled her large body up against the doorway. The doors always swing inward and it was virtually impossible to get someone out of the way of a door if they don't want to move. I tried to roll her out of the way but she just kept rolling back. We did this dance over and over as I pleaded with her to get the hell out of my apartment. There was a knock at the door. "Open up, it's the Police!" Thank god. Betty came to her senses and got up from the floor and doorway. Opening the door, I told them that this woman needed to be removed from my place. She just calmly walked out as if nothing happened. They looked around the apartment, saw the wreckage and asked me if I wanted to file a complaint. I said, "No." I figured it would just make her crazier and that was the last thing I needed.

Rob and my sister came back to the apartment and were surprised to see the TV smashed on the ground outside and the phone ripped out of the wall. After that,

Gina decided to go back to California and Rob moved to Winchester and stayed with his father. They couldn't take the drama anymore. I couldn't blame them. I was stuck dealing with Betty on my own. This episode seemed to revitalize her efforts to trap me again. She started coming over to my place all the time. Showing up at all hours, I couldn't stand it. When I wouldn't let her in she would bang on the door and scream at the top of her lungs in the hallway.

"Mark, you are a fucking asshole and don't take care of your daughter!"

My neighbors, obviously, started to freak out. Every time she showed up it felt like somebody held a death grip on my heart and just started squeezing. My chest felt like an elephant was standing on it. The worst part was that she brought Jasmine with her most of the time. I asked her, "Why are you arguing with me in front of Jasmine?" I begged her not to do that to Jasmine because of what I had gone through as a kid. I knew how it felt to be put in the middle of something ugly. She said she wanted Jasmine to see what kind of fucking bastard I was.

During this period of time, she finally snapped for real when I had a girl come over. The Beast had stalked me out in the parking lot, just watching to see if I was seeing anybody. This was the first time I went out on a date in months. The girl, Lori, left my apartment and I heard a knock on the door. I thought it was Lori and she had left something behind, so I didn't look through the peephole before opening the door. It was Betty.

She pushed the door open and went on a tirade. I saw blood in her eyes. The Beast charged and came at me like a wild animal, grabbing my hair with both hands. I could feel the absolute rage she had just by the grip she had on my hair. As much as possible, I tried to cover up my face, but she started punching me in my left eardrum. My head was ringing and she just cut loose, punch after punch. She opened up a cut over my eye and it started bleeding. I tried to get her to let go of my hair, but she had crazy strength in her hands that completely caught me off guard. She started ripping away at my face with her claws. Pain began shooting through me and I felt helpless. It felt like she was burning me with her fingernails. My face turned into a bloody mess.

I had blood all over the front of my shirt and she just wasn't letting up. The Beast caught me with a perfect punch that popped my eardrum. Instantly I saw red, that was it, I couldn't take it anymore and I finally drew my fist back and punched her as hard as I could. She went sprawling across the living room from the sheer force of the punch. She got up and with a sly, evil, psychotic grin just looked at me; she knew she had me. This was exactly what she wanted. I had finally physically harmed her and she would make me pay.

She turned around and left, and I knew I was in trouble. It was the first time I had ever laid my hands on a woman in anger and I knew I was going to suffer. As I looked at myself in the mirror, I looked like a raw piece of meat, but I knew that the law would side with a woman when it came to a domestic violence situation. It's hard to imagine that a former Marine could be assaulted by their wife.

I knew what was in store for me so I just waited for the police to arrive to arrest me. Within an hour they were there, knocking on my door, but surprisingly, she was with them. They saw what she had done to me, but informed me that Betsy had filed a restraining order on me. When I first heard him say it, I was ecstatic, because I knew she would have to stay away from me, as well. The last thing in the world I wanted was be around Betty so this was fantastic. Why in the world would she do this? It didn't make any sense to me. Then, he continued to tell me that I was going to have to leave my apartment. "What do you mean?" Officer Green said, "Your wife has listed this as her address." Stunned, I wasn't exactly sure what to say. "She doesn't live here. This isn't her place; this is my place!" Officer Green said that I'd have to take it up with the judge.

I begged them to come in and see that there were no women's clothing or items in my apartment. They just didn't care; it was a Friday night and I had no way of proving that this was my place and that Betty wasn't on the lease. I resigned myself to the fact that I had to leave. I walked out of my apartment after getting a few clothes and my toothbrush.

The Beast just walked in and smiled at me as she relished the victory. This bitch walked right into my apartment and there was nothing I could do about it. I ended up staying at the Continental Inn for the weekend. On Monday I went into the apartment manager's office, got a letter from her and a copy of my lease, and went down to the courthouse. The judge rescinded the restraining order and I was allowed to go back to my apartment. The amazing thing was that even though I had the proof that she had used the legal system and had filed a false report, the judge didn't do a damn thing about it. I began losing respect for the legal system from that moment on. The legal system is corrupt and does not look out for innocent people, and I learned a life lesson that I would carry with me from that moment on.

Betty had left a wake of destruction to let me know that she was there and that she was never going to let it go. Entering the apartment, it felt like I was walking into a war zone. She had cut open my living room couch and chair; stuffing hung out from everywhere and it was so bad, I couldn't even think about sitting on them anymore. The new TV and VCR were in pieces, scattered around on the floor.

Everything I owned in that apartment was destroyed; she left no stone unturned. My dishes, bowls, and glasses were in thousands of pieces and I couldn't even recognize most of the things in my apartment. "Oh my god," I thought out loud as I surveyed the wreckage. The Beast had to have taken her time and put a lot of work in over the weekend in order to do the damage she did. I'm sure her rage and psychotic nature fueled her and pushed her to destroy everything before she left.

I found my clothes and each item had been sliced with a knife, as had my mattress. Most clothes were cut directly in the crotch area. I imagine that she was sending me a pretty strong message and probably wanted to do that to my cock. Cut it right off. The most egregious action she took over that weekend really hit home and devastated me. She gathered up all of my Marine Corps uniforms, each medal and ribbon I had earned over my four years serving our country, and threw them in a pile. The Beast doused them with gasoline behind the back of my apartment complex. She lit a match and 'whoosh,' just like that, what represented my four years in the Marine Corps instantly went up in flames. When I finally saw the pile of burnt, melted ashes that used to be my uniforms I felt sick to my stomach, knowing there was no way of replacing any of those items, ever.

The Beast also found names of girls that I had gotten numbers from around my apartment. She gave each and every one of them a call, personally, to introduce herself as my wife and let them know that if they pursued any kind of relationship with me they would eventually meet her, and it wouldn't be pretty. I can only imagine the tone and seriousness of the message that was conveyed to those poor girls. The Beast didn't want any competition, though I wouldn't touch her if we were alone on the planet completely by ourselves. I never heard from a single one of those girls again, nor would they take my calls. She must have been pretty persuasive.

There I was, beaten to a pulp, black and blue from the beating I received from the Beast, in my wrecked apartment, surveying the full extent of the damage she had inflicted on my belongings and me. I had no idea what was next for me and felt vulnerable. Even though she didn't file assault charges, they took pictures of her where I had punched her and I now had a file on me down at the police station. This just sickened me to no end. I had never hit a woman in my entire life and now I'm known as an abuser. Betty went about destroying my reputation and told everyone in Lawrenceburg. She went into great detail on how I beat her up and how abusive I had been. Friends of mine called me and asked what was going on. They couldn't believe that I had changed so much as to start hitting on women. I was so mad and it sickened me that anyone believed the shit coming out of Betty's mouth. She was getting a lot of sympathy from people in Lawrenceburg and I looked like a total schmuck. For this reason, I stayed away from Lawrenceburg for a while because I didn't feel like explaining to people how fucking crazy she was. Most people didn't believe me anyway; no way could miss class president, miss 4.0 gpa throughout high school, be this psychotic bitch I described. I was finally fed up, quit trying to tell people I was innocent, and just let them think what they wanted.

Chapter 24

Rob and I worked at a factory in Frankfort making steel wheels for different car manufacturers. We both wanted to go to school and he came up with an idea that he sold me on. I had convinced him to join Marine Corps, so talked me into us going to school down in Eastern Kentucky, in Prestonsburg. This was a small coal mining community and the community college was extremely cheap. We could get our core classes out of the way and transfer back to the University of Kentucky. Rob had family in the area and I went down to meet them one weekend. Prestonsburg was about one hundred and fifty miles away from Lexington. We told his family our plan.

Desert Shield was in full swing at that time and I received a letter from the Marine Corps telling me to stand by. I could be recalled at any moment. For a second I got nervous that I was going to be recalled and have to return to active duty. Like everyone else, I had no idea what was going to happen over in the Middle East with Saddam Hussein. I just knew he was a crazy fucktard that tortured his own people. Back in that time, I just thought we should invade and destroy all of these radical countries that repressed their female population and tortured and killed their own citizens.

When I decided it was time to go to school and move, I brought this letter in and showed it to my boss at Topy, the factory where Rob and I worked. Rob and I enrolled at Prestonsburg Community College and I stopped showing up for work. I'm not sure why I just didn't quit, but I suppose I wanted to have a job available if I really needed it, just in case college didn't work out. The management of

Topy just assumed I was recalled back to active duty.

Of course, the main reason I wanted to get out of Lexington at that time was to get away from the Beast, just so I could breathe. I had grown so tired of dealing were her relentless bullshit and bringing my daughter around and fighting in front of her. That really bothered me, that Jasmine saw all of this shit. Betty was absolutely furious about me moving so far away. The nice thing was that I used her own words against her; I told her that I was going to college, like she had used against me in our phone conversations while I was in New York. I was doing what I said I would do. All that bullshit about me being more of a part of Jasmine's life had been a lie.

Enrolled in college and staying at Rob's uncle's house, I waited on Rob to show up, but for some reason, he never did. The plan was that we were going to stay with his uncle for a couple of weeks and then look for a place close to the college and split the rent. I was pretty excited to finally enroll in school. I really wanted to better my life and start the career I had in mind for myself.

Rob had a change of heart over the weekend and decided he wasn't going to go to school. I couldn't believe it; here I was staying with his family who I just barely knew and he didn't even tell me that he had changed his mind. I was stuck there for the time being. His uncle, aunt and cousins were great though and welcomed me in with open arms. They let me stay with them as long as I needed to in order to find a place to live.

In order to afford to go to college I applied for my GI bill money, financial aid and grants. I received $300 dollars a month from my GI bill and got a veteran's work-study job. They paid me minimum wage, $3.35 an hour. It sucked compared to my job in New York, but was enough to allow me to survive. The Beast had pressured me into giving her the truck I had bought and paid for once I returned from New York. It was a little sad as I had so many memories from the wild times spent with my Marine buddies. I went about looking for a cheap vehicle since I was going to school and didn't need an expensive car payment. I sent Betty $50 a week, which was all I could afford, to help out with Jasmine. Betty was used to all the money she used to get while I was in the Marine Corps. She used to get almost my entire check every month, but now things were tight. I went from making $1,000 a week in New York to making minimum wage. It was definitely a shock, but I was willing to sacrifice in order to go to school and get my degree. I thought having your college degree was the only way to get ahead in life.

Betty was pretty ticked that I wasn't close enough for her to come over and harass anymore so she thought she would harm me a different way. She actually had the nerve to take me to court to evaluate an increase in my child support.

At the time we never had anything on paper to how much I was giving her. I always gave as much as I could to make sure Jasmine was taken care of. She was pissed off about me moving and wanted to take me to the cleaners. Since I was only making $3.35 I didn't worry much about going to court and getting evaluated. We showed up for court and the judge demanded to see last year's tax returns. I gave them to him and explained that I had been working in New York and had quit that job to go to school and live closer to my daughter. I only make $3.35 an hour now and go to school fulltime. He responded, "Tough; if you were able to make this amount of money last year, then you can make it this year!" Our fucking legal system at work again. There was no way I could make that kind of money in Kentucky while trying to go to school full time. He set my child support at more than I was bringing home each week.

The one thing I knew for sure was that Betsy didn't want me going anywhere, so I told her that this was going to force me to go back to New York so I could make the money to pay child support. I did a great job for the mobsters in New York so I knew they would take me back in a second. This was absolutely the last thing she wanted. She wanted to hurt me, but hadn't really thought this move through thoroughly. The Beast didn't want me out of her radar screen. I told her that I made a call to New York and they would be happy to have me back. This gave me the leverage to work out a compromise. I didn't want to go back to New York, as I really wanted to go to school, and she didn't want me to leave the state, so she went and had the child support lowered to where I could afford to pay it and stay in school. This was one time I used her obsessive-compulsive nature against her. She wouldn't know what to do without me there to obsess over. It taught me a great lesson and I started to learn how to play the game with Betty. She was still the master, but I was learning.

I began my college career and worked at the Veterans Referral Center in Paintsville. It was a really rewarding place to do work-study. The guys who hung around this place were a different type of breed. Almost all of them were Vietnam veterans. Almost every one of them wore camouflage still, and always packed a gun of some sort. These guys were paranoid as hell. I guess I would be too if I had gone through some of the things they had been through in Vietnam. I worked for a guy named John Chef who was the counselor and had written the grant in order to open up the center for the veterans. He was also a Vietnam vet, so he had a keen insight into what made these guys tick. Mostly, my job was to assist veterans in getting their benefits from the government. I did this by helping them fill out the proper forms and gave them a place to hang out.

They enjoyed giving me a bunch of shit all the time. Since I was newly discharged from the Marine Corps I would always hear the 'back when I was in' stories and how easy I had it, compared to them. I enjoyed working with these guys. I had a true respect for what they had done and how our country really hadn't supported them. You could tell how twisted they were when Halloween came around. They would put on a haunted house and people from all over the state would come to it. Word got out on how far they would go in order to scare the shit out of people. They went all out. These guys had real chain saws going, of course, without the chain and wrapped in duct tape. Still, realistic as could be. They had pig intestines and real blood all over them as they went around scaring the hell out of people. I hadn't seen a haunted house as graphic or as scary, ever.

I settled in and spent the majority of my time going to school, studying, and working at the referral center. I found a place to live in within walking distance, right next to the college. A very eccentric high school teacher in Prestonsburg owned it. He had a water wheel attached to his house and in the back, a tugboat that he had converted to an apartment and a small A-frame. I rented out the A-frame and thought it was cool to live in one. It felt like I was living in a fort like a kid, and it reminded me of the party trailer off the base that I had for a while. It was no bigger than a small trailer, but I was happy with it and slept upstairs in the loft. Cozy is the word I would use to describe it. It had a small kitchen area, living room, and my mattress was upstairs in the loft. I started making friends with people in my classes and at the referral center.

Rob decided to come down and hang out for the weekend. We decided to go out to a local club on a Friday night. This was the only nightclub around in a 50-mile area so everybody that was single went there. It was packed. One girl got my attention; she had no make-up on and was not trying to get attention. She had a pair of jeans and a sweatshirt on, not too sexy in the dressing department, but had this angelic look about her. She was absolutely beautiful and I couldn't take my eyes off of her. She was about 5'6" and 108 = pounds with beautiful blonde hair and a great smile. Her skin was tan and you could tell she was really fit under her clothes.

I thought it was amazing that she was absolutely gorgeous and didn't even know it, or at least, didn't express that she knew. Most times I wasn't afraid at all to talk to women. But it took me a minute or so to finally muster up the courage to approach her. I had caught her eye, as well. She stared at me as I crossed the room to talk to her. Just then, a new song came on and somebody asked her to dance, right before I got to her. She said yes and walked off with this guy. I was crushed, until she turned around, looked back at me and gave me a small smile. I guess she was playing hard to get. Finally I got to talk to her after she finished dancing with that clown. Her name was Brenda and she had come down from Morehead State with a bunch of her friends. Morehead was about 65 miles away.

She instantly took me in; we had this amazing

chemistry right off the bat. We spent the rest of the night talking and dancing. Other than the first time I tried to talk with her, everything was perfect. I think it was love at first sight for me. Unfortunately one of her friends had a little too much to drink and she had to leave way too early for my taste. I helped Brenda take her friend to the car and laid on an incredible goodnight kiss that made her knees buckle. It filled my stomach with butterflies; I couldn't believe how excited I was to meet this girl. She gave me her number and I promised to call. All she kept saying all night was that she couldn't believe anybody even approached her because of what she was wearing. She thought she looked terrible.

Brenda could never look terrible if she tried. I called her the next day and we made plans to get together the following weekend. After our first date, we became inseparable and spent as much time as possible together. She was having trouble at Morehead with her grades and the financing so she had to drop out. Her father was a tobacco farmer and couldn't afford to keep her in school anymore. Brenda was 18 and I had just turned 23. She moved back home to Campton, a tiny little town in eastern Kentucky about 40 minutes from me.

She began staying with her aunt because she wasn't getting along with her parents. We spent as much time together as possible. I wasn't making much money so we weren't able to do anything extravagant, but we always had a good time together. The first time we made love it was amazing. I knew I loved her and she had never been with a real man before, so she was amazed at the things I did to her. She had only slept with teenage boys until this point, so I was a complete shock for her. We were both hooked, instantly.

We had one major setback that almost ended our relationship. We decided to go out to the nightclub where we first met with Rob and his cousin, Jackie. The club was really lax when it came to checking IDs and if you had cover money, nine times out of ten you got in. It wasn't difficult and we were able to get her in. She had a fake ID and I don't think they checked very hard, anyway. So, we all started to have fun and a few cocktails. This was one of the first times that we had drank alcohol together and I didn't know it, but Brenda couldn't handle her liquor very well. Within no time she was absolutely smashed. This caused her to act really strange. She said she was going to the ladies room and would be right back. After she had been gone for a little while I started to look around for her. I spotted her leaning against a wall by herself. I went over and told her to come sit down; she responded that she would be over in a minute. She was really hammered. I left her there and went back to the table.

The next time I saw her she was on the dance floor with some mullet wearing redneck, slow dancing. She had her head down a bit and I knew she was wasted. I didn't care about her dancing with this guy until I saw him groping all over her ass. Of course I'm not going to let some guy grope all over my girlfriend's ass so I went to where they were dancing. I said, "Hey buddy, this is my girlfriend and she has had too much to drink so I'm taking her home." He looked at me and responded, "Hey, it looks like she is with me, asshole!" I felt the anger inside me as my blood pressure raised. Trying hard to keep my temper in check, I calmly told him that I was responsible for her and that I'm taking her home. He turned and said, "You have a fucking problem; do you want to go outside?" This guy had no idea how much he had chewed off; I was furious at this point and would teach him the lesson of his life.

Brenda stood there acting like an idiot and not saying one word. I told the hillbilly, redneck asshole in a very soft voice "I'd love to." We both made our way through the crowd to the door, as I followed behind him. This poor guy didn't know what hit him. As soon as we got outside I threw him up against a truck really hard, as I was super pissed and really strong. He bounced off the truck and ran right into my fist, hitting as hard as I had ever hit anybody. "Thud!!" his knees immediately buckled and his eyes rolled back into his head. His body just slumped to the ground. I had knocked him unconscious with one punch.

Instantly, without any warning, I was hit from behind by three big, corn-fed bouncers from the bar. They slammed me up against the truck and I fell to the ground on my knees. They pinned me underneath the truck and started hammering away with their boots, kicking me as many times as they could. I covered up the best I could, but they continued to kick me in the face, ribs, and balls; everywhere. I remember just being angry as they continued kicking the shit out of me. I didn't feel any pain, just anger. The guy I knocked out was still on the ground and no one had even started helping him; they were more pre-occupied with giving me a beating. They were gutless wonders, I thought, as they had tackled me from behind.

They finally got tired and left me there to bleed. Slowly, I made my way to my knees and eventually was able to stand up, trying to get my myself together. My head throbbed as I felt the pulse coming from my temple. I definitely felt disoriented walking around outside in the parking lot, outside the club. All of a sudden I see Brenda outside, leaning up against a wall. I'm bleeding pretty badly from a cut over my eye, walk over to her and start yelling at her.

"You stupid bitch! Do you see my face? You caused this!"

At that moment, one of the bouncers who had been kicking me came up and tried to get in the middle of my argument with Brenda. Instantly I recognized him and my eyes became red with rage. He made a big mistake coming up to me on his own. I reared back and punched him right in the nose; he stumbled over a piece of cement and hit the ground. I absolutely lost it. As he lay on the ground I went over and started kicking him in the side of his ribs as he tried to cover up. "How do you like it, mother fucker! How do you like it?" I yelled over and over. He got ahold of his radio and screamed like a little girl for somebody to come and help him. "Help me, help me!" he called out repeatedly.

Every bouncer in the place came running out to the parking lot. I finally stopped kicking him and found myself completely surrounded by all of his comrades. These guys had ill will in their eyes; each of them had mag light flashlights and moved in on me. I was so full of rage and wound up from what happened that I didn't even care.

"I promise that I will sue and press charges on anyone that hits me with one of those fucking flashlights!"

I couldn't believe the shit that was coming out of my mouth. "I'm going to sue this place and every one of you will be fired!" I tried to think of anything to keep these guys off me. They all stopped in their tracks and didn't press on me further. I was ready to fight and die right there.

The lead bouncer finally said, "Just get the hell out of here!" I didn't look back; I left the parking lot and just walked home. Later on that evening Rob dropped Brenda off at my house and I went out to get her from his car. She had passed out; no surprise there. I carried her in and put her on the couch. As I laid her down I swore to myself that I would drive her home and never see her again in the morning. My left eye was completely swollen and closed in the morning. Dried streaks of blood ran down my face and neck and my shirt looked like I had been in the fight of my life. I couldn't believe what had happened last night. In all of my fights growing up, I had never looked like this.

I woke Brenda up and told her to get her things. "I'm taking you home and I never want to see you again," I told her. She started crying and begged me not to take her home. She was so sorry and would never drink like that again if I just gave her another chance. I wasn't in the mood to be so forgiving and told her, "No, get your shit; I'm taking you home." She knew it was over if I was able to get her home so she told me how much she loved me and that she would never do anything to hurt me again. I finally calmed down and she cleaned all of my cuts and iced my bruises. She took care of me while I recovered and we put that crazy episode behind us.

From that point on she basically moved in with me. We had known each other for about two months and just couldn't stand to be away from each other, so we started living together and making plans for the future. I told her what my dream was; I wanted to finish school and work on Wall Street. I wanted to make the kind of money I was making in New York; even more. I never wanted to be poor again and wanted to live the life that rich, successful people had. My plan was to get an education and a job that had unlimited earning potential. Brenda wasn't sure what she wanted to do and I told her that was okay because I had no clue right when I got out of high school, either. We decided that she would enroll at PCC and take basic core classes like I was until she decided what she wanted to do.

Finally I felt happy, living so far away from the Beast, having a girlfriend and going to school. This was one of the happiest times of my life. I was broke, but had enough to squeak by and pay my bills, pay my child support, go to school and just be loved by this amazing person. Brenda and I ended up having a few classes together so I would help her with her class work. In a real lucky break for us she got a job as a DJ within walking distance of our A-frame. It was cool to hear her on the radio. Her little brother, "Bub," bragged about his sister to all his friends while he was in junior high school. He told them to listen to his sister on the radio, he had a celebrity for a sister. I thought this was truly funny, but was pretty proud of her, too. She got along great with all the guys at the veteran's referral center. They absolutely loved when she was around; she was so pretty and just had this quality about her that everyone responded to.

Eventually. the Beast found out about my new love. She threatened to come down to Prestonsburg and break us up. Our relationship had already reached a point that Betty had no chance making that happen. And luckily, I hadn't told her exactly where I lived. She was crazy and resourceful enough to find me, somehow, so I knew that our location was just temporarily. Of course, Betty lost it. As usual, she wanted her and I to get back together. Brenda was a real threat. The Beast was able to chase away many girls in Lexington before I was able to get close to anybody, but Brenda had already moved in with me.

Betty started to call obsessively again and there was no slowing her down. She called me at the referral center

10 times a day, demanding to speak with me. We talked in circles, as usual. "Mark, we need to talk." I always asked, "About what, now?" She always went back to how we needed to work things out for Jasmine's sake and that we needed to be together. I tried to get her mental help a long time ago, but she just scoffed at me. She thought that she had acted just as normal as could be. The Beast had attempted suicide on three different occasions. How normal does she think she is?

There was no getting through to her, and since the referral center was a public place, she would call and call and call. My boss saw what I was going through and tried to intercept as many phone calls as possible. Everyone at the referral center knew about my crazy wife and tried to shield me from her, but Betty got creative on occasion. She would pretend to be somebody else and they would patch her through to me. I was so disgusted to have to deal with this when I knew what it felt like to love somebody like Brenda. My detest for Betty grew daily. She thought this would work. I was perplexed that somebody could think that if you torture someone long enough they will lose the will to fight you and just cave in. I suppose her philosophy came from the time she had done it early in our relationship and it worked. She would call and wake me up in the morning and continue to call all day long. She kept this up until I changed my phone number. She always came up with something like, "What if Jasmine has an emergency and I can't get ahold of you?" as to why she needed my phone number. I told her that she could have it if she stopped calling me unless it was about Jasmine.

Of course, she would agree to this and not call for a week, but then it would resume like normal. Brenda and I unhooked the phone if we didn't want to hear it ring. I jumped every time it rang, affected by the years of phone stalking. My heart skipped every time a phone rang, no matter where I was. I knew it had to be Betty tracking me, wanting to talk to me. I decided I wasn't going to talk to her anymore. Anytime I heard her voice I immediately hung up. This truly infuriated her and the game went on for a little while. She called my home all day long, and I picked up the phone and hung it up.

Somehow she found out where Brenda worked. I never figured out how she got her information. She was amazing at tracking and finding out what she wanted. I had never told her where I worked but she was able to find out. I never questioned Betty's intelligence. She was incredibly smart. Absolutely frustrated that I wouldn't talk to her on the phone, she started to call Brenda at the radio station. Brenda was so sweet, she still was very patient with Betty. I happened to be there when Betty started calling the station. The radio station was right next door to our place so I would hang out with Brenda when I could. Betty called and told Brenda that she wanted to speak with me and I waved my hand to say no.

The Beast talked to Brenda for hours on end normally but on this day, Brenda told Betty that I didn't want to talk with her and hung up. Betty called back seven more times. Each time, Brenda conveyed the message that I wouldn't speak to her. I had managed not to speak to Betty in over three weeks. I believe that was the longest time period I went without talking to the Beast since I was in the Marine Corps on a deployment. On the last phone call, Betty told Brenda that if I didn't speak to her, I would be sorry. I told Brenda that I wasn't going to speak with her no matter what.

We didn't hear from Betty, and one day, while I was at

work at the veteran's referral center, the sheriff came in looking for me. To my utter shock and disgust, he had an arrest warrant for me. Betty snapped on the day that I refused to talk to her, similarly to when I was in Okinawa. She had gone down to the police station in Lawrenceburg and filed a complaint against me. It was amazing but she alleged that I had threatened to kill her and kidnap my daughter when we talked on the phone on the day in question. Since I hadn't spoken with her at all I couldn't believe that I was being arrested. The small town that Lawrenceburg was, the sheriff who took her complaint was somebody she had graduated high school with, Henry Crown. His father was the real sheriff; he was just a deputy sheriff. He knew she was full of shit but had to take the complaint, by law. This was a felony offense I was facing. Terroristic threatening of a witness and attempted kidnapping were the charges levied against me. Betty's family was influential in Lawrenceburg's politics so I had reason to be afraid. The sheriff told me he had to take me in. My boss, John Chef, knew this was bogus because everyone at the center knew how psychotic Betty was, by just calling as much as she did. John was a counselor to Vietnam vets, so he knew the signs and had told me a long time ago that Betty had a bipolar personality and was dangerous.

My bail was set at $500 dollars. It might as well have been $5,000 dollars. I had no money to bail myself out of jail. Thank god John came and got me. I was pretty shaken up, riding to jail knowing I hadn't done anything wrong and that they can put you in jail without any proof, any evidence, nothing. Just Betty's word that I said these things. Another lesson about our justice system. I was so mad sitting there on the cold cement floor, knowing that Betty had done this to me. If I could have gotten ahold of her right then, I believe I would have killed her and not regretted it one bit. I would have been happy to spend the rest of my life in jail for the satisfaction of ridding the world of this crazy, evil bitch. I froze my ass off all night long. They didn't have a judge to allow John or I to post bail so I spent the night in jail. I was looking at a possible five-year prison sentence if she was able to convince a jury I had done this. It was sickening how distorted our legal system is.

That is exactly what Betty wanted. She would have me put away so I couldn't be with Brenda anymore. I wouldn't be able to be with any woman and she would be able to come see me in jail and send me letters. I had a real problem on my hands given the prosecuting attorney filed a felony complaint against me. This was a serious matter, and the Lawrenceburg court system was corrupt. It was a good old boys' club. Betty's uncle was one of the good old boys. The prosecutors were a married couple. The husband was known to be connected with drug dealers in Lawrenceburg so I had no idea what I was getting myself in to.

I decided to hire a lawyer from Lexington, though I did most of the preparation for my defense and strategized how to take down the Beast. My lawyer's name was Jessica Knight and she was awesome. Brenda and I went to see her. We sat down and told Jessica what had been going on in great detail. I went through my experiences in the Marine Corps, the constant phone calls, Betty's attempted suicides and everything else I could think of to give Jessica the entire picture. I told her about Lawrenceburg and Betty's family influence in the court system. She told me not to worry. I couldn't help but worry; this was my entire future. My heart pounded that first day as I walked up the stairs to the courthouse. So ironic that they were the same exact stairs I had walked up when I stupidly caved and married the Beast. I had Brenda by my side and that gave me some comfort, but I was absolutely terrified at the thought of losing everything. I had absolutely no faith in our legal system. We were all called to order and it began. On the first day of the trial Betty was called to the stand by the absolute bitch of a prosecuting attorney. The Beast was in rare form; she gave an incredible performance on the stand. She reiterated the fact that she was so frightened of me. She feared for her life and worried about Jasmine. It was absolutely sickening. Just listening to her spew lie after lie made my stomach churn. It was so surreal and I began to panic as her lies became more descriptive. Brenda held my hand and I felt I could make it through this.

Betty's mother was in the courtroom and I looked at her with disgust. She knew I wasn't capable of this. She knew her daughter was a liar but she sat there and supported her. I use to have such respect for her mother and felt love for her; it was gone from that moment on. Why wouldn't she talk Betty out of doing this? This could destroy my life. Betty's mom was a Christian and just sat there quietly, letting her daughter lie after swearing on a bible. Betty, of course, was phony, too. She attended church religiously, every week, while torturing me all these years. What a fucking hypocrite. They both were. The prosecuting attorney finished asking Betty questions about how much of a danger I was after laying it on thick. This was the moment I was waiting for. I had written up detailed notes on each and every event that I could prove where the Beast had done something egregious. She did not know what was getting ready to hit her. From the crazy phone calls, to her attempted suicides, it was all going to come out and I would have my day in court. My attorney stood up, armed with my notes and specific questions that I had coached her to ask in preparation for the big day. Jessica also was armed with another exceptional piece of evidence that would be a game changer.

Jessica began with a simple question. "Betty, you say that Mark called you and threatened you on the day in question; is that correct?" Betty replied, "Yes."

"Well, Mrs. Milano, I have a copy of your phone record and a copy of Mark's phone record for the date in question. It appears that Mark called you... hmm, well it looks like Mark never called you that day. In fact, I have Mark's phone record for the previous two months. He hasn't called you, ever. Can you explain this to the court?" Betty responded, "No."

"Well, let's take a look at your phone record for the day in question. It appears that you called Mark's number 76 times that day. And then you called his girlfriend's radio station eight more times.-Now tell me, Mrs. Milano, if you were so afraid of Mark and what he might do, why would you keep calling so many times?"

Betty was stunned. She hadn't thought about how she would look when the facts came out. She just wanted to hurt me. She wouldn't answer the question. The prosecuting attorneys sat with their mouths wide open. I guess they hadn't imagined that Betty might be full of shit. Amazingly, using the taxpayers' money, they hadn't bothered to do any investigative work on this felony case. For someone so potentially dangerous that they were trying to convey to the judge, I was shocked that our prosecuting attorneys were so inept. These two morons were so pathetically unintelligent for people who had actually passed the bar exam.

Jessica went on to ask Betty, "Mrs. Milano, how many times have you attempted suicide in the past few years?" Betty's eyes instantly went right at me; she just stared at me. I felt the hatred and anger; it was like daggers shot out of her eyes. The Beast was finally rocked and having a hard time trying to keep composed on the stand. Jessica had really gotten to her. Betty knew she couldn't lie about the suicide attempts. They were well documented and she knew it. The Red Cross had a record of each time I went on emergency leave and what the nature of the emergency was. So, she answered, "I think three."

The judge interrupted Jessica and put a halt to the fiasco of a trial. He knew the case was bogus and that the prosecuting attorneys hadn't done their homework. He dismissed it, right then and there. The judge actually gave the prosecuting attorneys an earful for their lack of preparation, not knowing any of the real facts of the case and wasting the people's time. Oh my god, I felt such relief. The weight of the world came off my back. I took a breath for what felt like the first time in months. Betty was so bitter. Her face was red with anger. Her plan hadn't worked; she wasn't able to put me in jail or make me suffer through a long court hearing. But the worst thing was that I would still be with Brenda. I grabbed Brenda as I saw Betty out of the corner of my eye, pulled her close, put my mouth on her and gave her the most passionate kiss I could muster at the time. The Beast was enraged; if we weren't right in the middle of the courthouse she probably would have attacked Brenda and I right there. In the long run, she had hurt me, though. I hadn't slept in months waiting for the court date to finally come. Financially, it crushed me as well; I had to pay Jessica $1,500 dollars. This was an incredible amount of money for somebody making minimum wage.

The stress of waiting to see if you're going to go to jail or go free is enormous. I would have felt better if I was guilty. Then I wouldn't feel bad if I was convicted. But to know this was a lie and that my whole future was on the line because of this lying bitch caused me many sleepless nights. Brenda and I breathed a sigh of relief and headed back to Prestonsburg. I told Jessica she was the most impressive lawyer I had ever seen. It felt so good to see Betty on that stand, squirming, her psychotic actions out there on display for the world to see. She had never paid the price for anything she had done to me at that point. It was nice to see her feel some shame. It also felt good to show her mother how crazy her daughter was and how much of a liar she was. Jessica was so worth the money.

Chapter 25

I started filing for divorce as soon as I got back to Prestonsburg. I had put it off due to finances but no matter what, I was getting a divorce. As soon as papers reached Betty she went and filed for divorce as well. She was worried I would bring up all the things she had done over the history of our marriage in court so she wanted to strike first. I just wanted to finally be rid of her once and for all, legally. I let her hire the attorney and pay for the divorce. I didn't have many possessions at this point in my life, so whatever she asked for, I just gave her. The only thing I wanted, I had, and that was Brenda. Betty had never been small to begin with but had really packed on the weight since she became pregnant with Jasmine. She hadn't quit eating for two. Brenda was the exact opposite; she was slender and looked like a fitness model. Every time Betty saw her I could tell by the look in her eye that she absolutely hated Brenda with every fiber of her being. I was going to give her the truck I had paid for and was going to keep my cheap car. She got everything else I had of value. I didn't care. I knew I could start again. They were just possessions, anyway.

Betty hadn't done anything with her life the entire time we were married. Gone to school, had a job, nothing. She only lived to make my life miserable. Besides taking care of Jasmine she spent all of her time thinking of ways to terrorize me. That is way too much time for anybody to be obsessed. She finally got a job; my $50 dollars a week wasn't enough money for her to just sit at home and live the good life. I was happy to see her get off her lazy ass and finally do something productive. Unfortunately, she loaned her truck to a friend of hers and they wrapped it around a tree. We hadn't finalized our divorce yet so she told me that she wanted my car. I told her to fuck off but she countered that she would drag out our divorce indefinitely unless I gave her my car.

I wanted to be divorced from her so badly I would have cut off my arm to make it happen. I came up with a compromise; I had excellent credit so I would help her buy a car because I couldn't afford to go out and buy another car myself. My budget was extremely tight but my credit was good. She made decent money so I told her to find a car and I would get it for her, but she would have to pay for it. I wanted this in writing, in our divorce papers. She agreed to the request. She found a car and I bought it for her. She never made one payment; surprising, huh? I tried my best to keep up with both payments but couldn't do it. She really fucked me now.

My credit was going in the tank, she was driving around in a free car and Brenda was stressed about everything Betty was putting us through. I finally called the bank and told them that I just couldn't make the payments, for them to come and get the car. Betty was furious. She had justified to herself that she was entitled to the car for all the emotional pain I had caused her and that I should pay for it. I just couldn't afford it, making minimum wage and going to school full time. She then insisted that I give her my car or she would ask for child support to be raised back to where it was. She knew I was in school and that Brenda and I lived together, so I really didn't want to go back to New York and agreed to let her have my car. Brenda and I scrambled to find some car to get us around before I had to give Betty mine. We finally found some beat up junker that ran ok and bought it. Poor Brenda had to put up with so much just to be with me. It was a lot to handle for someone 19 years old. She floored me one day when she said that she wanted to get married. After what I just went through, I had never planned on getting married again! But, she stood by me the entire time and I loved her so much that I had a hard time convincing myself that I didn't want to marry her. So, after much thought, I asked her to marry me.

We got married behind her parents' house. I felt this warm energy run through my hand as I held hers, as we prepared to give our vows. This is what love is supposed to be. I couldn't believe somebody could put up with all of the shit Betty had put me through. I was shocked that this beautiful, sweet girl wanted to marry me. I had all of these plans to finish college and start a career on Wall Street. I wanted to be rich; I knew that people who said money is the root of all evil just plain didn't have any. I knew the ramifications of having money in our society versus not having money. Having been taught a lesson by the legal system had opened my eyes and made me driven to an extent that I would be successful and rich or die trying. It felt much better when I was in New York and had the money to hire an attorney on a whim to deal with the Beast. Having no money and being broke gives you no power or respect in our society. I was on a mission to overcome the financial duress Betty had put me in.

Since I had given Betty my car I wanted her to put it into her name. She just wouldn't do it. I must have asked her 20 times to change the title. I would be liable if she was in an accident and hurt or killed someone. Of course, she was fine with having my ass on the line. I racked my brain on how to get her to change the title into her name. A veteran at the referral center came up with an idea. He told me to take the license plate off the car I had given her. I thought that was brilliant! She would have to drive around without a license plate and couldn't get one herself because the car was still in my name. I initiated my plan. I was going to have to call someone in that I could trust, someone I would take a bullet for. I brought in my best friend and Marine brother, Rob, to take on the mission. There wasn't a whole lot of strategic planning involved. We decided to pick a night during the week in which the Beast would be in bed early. We settled on a Tuesday. Rob and I dressed up in all black like cat burglars. Black pants and a black hoodie with a beanie for good measure. We drove to Betty's apartment complex around midnight. Carefully, we drove by my car and then circled back one more time to make sure no one was around to see what we were doing. I parked the car two blocks away and we got out. Staying out of the lights, we made our way to the parking lot. Rob stood guard as I made my way to my car. I bent down, grabbed the license plate and pulled hard. It took a few seconds before it finally gave way. Finally, it broke free; the license plate was in my hands. We quickly made our way back to the car and got in. My grand plan was to take the license plate out to Rob's dad's farm and bury it. I have no idea why I felt the need to bury it but we did and now Betty would be driving around without legal plates.

A few days went by and I started getting phone calls from the Beast. "Mark, I need you to sign those papers to transfer the car over." I was laughing so hard knowing that she now felt the heat. She had been pulled over already and did not like the answer the police officer gave her when she said it wasn't her car. I saw she had a lost tag sign in the back of the car now. I absolutely loved it! I took my sweet time and didn't call her back. The phone calls got more and more desperate. She had been stopped a number of times now for driving around without plates. Kind of an easy target for the Lexington Police Department. Lexington appears to have more cops per capita than anywhere else I have ever lived. Finally, after the fifth time she had been pulled over, the Beast was taken into custody and arrested. Unfortunately, she had my daughter with her at the time. I felt bad that Jasmine had to endure her mother being arrested but some part of me really enjoyed the fact that she was taken into custody. The Beast was getting a little bit of her own medicine.

Finally, I took her phone call and she stressed how much she needed me to sign papers to get the car registered in her name. I asked what happened and she told me that someone had stolen the car plates. I asked, "Who would do such a thing? I wonder why someone would take your license plate?" It was all I could do to keep it together and not laugh my ass off. She couldn't pick up on the slight sarcasm in my voice. I wanted to tell her so badly that it was me that took those plates off and that I was the reason she had been going through hell over the past month, but I took the cautious way out and set up a time to meet and sign over the registration. I couldn't help but say, "Hey, I have been trying to get this registration signed over for a while now, Betty". She didn't say anything and I went on my merry way. It was the first victory I had over the Beast the whole nightmare time I had known her. So sad and pathetic, that was my one and only victory.

Things finally started to settle down a bit for Brenda and I. We got a reprieve from Betty's antics for a while. I focused on school and work and tried to have some sort of normalcy in my life. It wasn't too long before the Beast started her antics again.

In our divorce, I had my visitation agreement written

219

out very specifically because I knew the Beast would try to fuck with me in regards to seeing my daughter. What the court system (as well as everyone else that pretends to know what they are talking about when it comes to the visitation of your child) misses is that those rules they put into place are made for normal, nonpsychotic people. When dealing with a crazy person the laws just don't cut it.

I arrived to pick up my daughter for my scheduled weekend and the Beast answered the door. I could tell by the look on her face that I was in for some sort of typical craziness. I asked her if Jasmine was ready and packed for the weekend and her response was, "I spoke with Jasmine, she doesn't feel like going with you this weekend and I'm not going to make her." I had just driven over 100 miles to pick her up and was stunned. I gathered myself and tried to remain calm. "Betty, just go get her, I don't want any trouble; I just want to have my daughter for the weekend." I was rebuffed again and Jasmine was nowhere to be seen. I wasn't even sure she was in the apartment. Going back and forth with the Beast just sucks and I knew I wasn't going to win the battle. I told her I was going to the police with my written visitation order if she didn't get Jasmine. She told good luck and me to go ahead.

I drove down to the police station and spoke with a police officer. I described what was going on and that it was my weekend with my daughter. He said he would send a couple of police officers to the Beast's apartment to supervise the exchange. I walked up to the door with the police officers and the Beast answered the door, all smiles. She said, "Officers, please come in," and for the next 15 minutes, I stood outside while she put on some sort of show. Needless to say, the cops came out and gave me a look of disgust. Who knows what the fucking Beast said to them. I was used to her being able to snow people over. One officer said, "Please don't waste our time anymore, Sir, your ex-wife said that she has your daughter ready to go and that it was just a miscommunication between you two." She looked at me the entire time with the fucking smirk she had mastered to perfection.

As soon as they left she said, "She isn't going and go get the police again if you want." She laughed and shut the apartment door in my face. I was absolutely pissed but knew she had me. Beaten, I got back in my car and started the long trip back to Eastern Kentucky. The taste of defeat fresh, I knew she had control, no matter what some piece of paper said. She would always control and dictate my relationship with my daughter.

I took a break for a while from seeing my daughter. I didn't have the fortitude or stamina to deal with the impenetrable wall of the Beast. I settled in to working, going to school and living life with Brenda. I spent a great deal of time at my work-study program and going to school.

Eventually, after a year I made my way back to Lexington, and at that time, tried to reestablish a relationship with my daughter. It was tough to actually deal with the enormous financial nightmare Betty had created for us, especially for someone as young at the time as Brenda. We had a hard time paying our bills and rent. Betty had waged such a war on my life from so many angles and it finally caught up to me. I tried to hold everything together but eventually, it became too much to bear for Brenda. One of the saddest days of my life started with her saying, "Mark, I can't be with you anymore; I am going to move back home with my family." It absolutely devastated me. I thought my heart would stop right then and there. She had stood by me through all of the horrible things the Beast had done. It was hard to get my head around her giving up now. She was still a baby at 20; what could I expect? In all actuality, she had hung in there so long I really had no right to expect any more out of her, but I couldn't get my heart to stop hurting.

Brenda packed her things and her parents came to pick her up. When she walked out the door, I felt a part of me left and my life crumbled in around me. I had many dark days for the next few months. My shit job was all I had. I worked in the same factory that made aluminum cast wheels and the temperature sometimes got to 150 degrees during the summer. I became really close to a co-worker that tried to help me through this very tough time in my life. Danny was older and much wiser than I was. He had big, white hair and a full, white beard. He knew the kind of pain I was in and no matter how much I talked about it, was patient and still lent that understanding ear. He happened to be in a semi-famous rock band that had converted to a country band quite a few years prior to when I met him. He never advertised it but I found out when he invited me to dinner with him, his wife and their newborn baby. A door to the closet opened up and there he was in a button-down shirt, his full chest exposed down to his belly, no beard but the long hair most seventies rockers had. I was stunned when I saw his poster and it made me realize that you can't judge a book by its cover. It helped to have a friend that had been there and done that. After a few months, my heart felt like it was starting to function again and I could breathe once more.

Jasmine came sporadically and spent some weekends with me. She must have mentioned to Betty that she didn't see Brenda at my place anymore. Betty somehow got verification from someone, knew that Brenda had left me, and was all too ready to pounce. This was absolutely the last thing I needed and I really felt sick to my stomach when I got the call from the Beast. "Mark, I'm sorry to hear that things haven't worked out for you and Brenda." Fucking pathetic; she caused most of our issues and I was heartbroken.

Unfortunately for Betty I was wiser, older and would never be manipulated by her again. She started terrorizing me at my apartment again, showing up unannounced with Jasmine, banging on my door, wanting to see me. Bang, bang, bang. "Mark, I know you are in there! Let me in; we should talk." All I could do was ignore her and let her stay outside with Jasmine. I felt like an asshole leaving my daughter outside hearing all of this but knew it would be much worse if I opened that door and see the wrath of a newly scorned Beast.

This power struggle went on for a while and my dating life absolutely sucked. I was terrified to ever let someone date me and have to deal with the Beast. I knew she would never let me be with someone again. Brenda was a mistake on her part; she needed to keep closer watch of my life so I wouldn't try and love, or be loved, by another woman ever again.

I went through a tough stage during this time. In a lot of ways I wasn't ready to let my guard down and let someone in, and then on top of that, I had the Beast waging her war against my love life. I met a married woman who was not happy with her husband, but had kids and didn't want to leave him. We started an affair and for me, it was perfect because I knew she couldn't break my heart nor could she judge me if my psycho ex showed up at my door. Kim had me come over to her house when her husband went into work. He worked third shift and left her home with the kids. Kim was quite pretty and had long, dark, brunette hair with a great body that was quite athletic. She was insatiable and never turned me down. In fact, most times she wore a skirt or dress with no panties on. Kim loved how I would just take her when I walked through the door. She needed the attention she lacked in her relationship with her husband and I needed to feel a connection, even a small one, with someone. Our relationship lacked depth, but we got what we needed from each other. At one time, I started talking to her about leaving her husband and us taking a shot with each other but quickly found out that she didn't think about me in that capacity in the least. Kind of hurt my feelings, but I knew it was virtually impossible for me to give any part of my heart to anyone at that time.

All the while Betty kept trying to get me while I was single. She grew more and more frustrated though she never saw me with any girls. I never dared bring anyone home. I lived in absolute fear that Betty would know and show up banging on my door until she scared them off.

Chapter 26

Betty began to really get frustrated at the thought of never getting back together with me and she wanted to teach me a lesson. She had tried to use the military against me, the court system against me, but she just couldn't make me suffer enough for her liking.

She had some thuggish friends at that time and didn't mind getting them involved in hurting me. The Beast had reached a point of wanting to inflict some pain on me as she felt I deserved it for putting her through hell as all she had done since we were teenagers was to love me. Her 'friend' Bobby was 6'2" and weighed in around 200 pounds. He sported a retro 80's mullet that he thought was still cool (though it never was). He had trashy tattoos that he might have drawn himself, they were so bad. Drew had a similar build, but not the sweet mullet Bobby sported. Betty had worked them into a frenzy telling them some very detailed stories of my physical abuse and how I hadn't paid for my transgressions by the legal system for what I had done to her and my daughter. At this point, they were determined to teach me a lesson. She let them know where I lived and when I would most likely be home.

I sat having a relaxing evening, watching a movie, when I heard a knock at the door. The knocking became louder and louder and I became a little pissed from its aggressive nature. I started to open the door; these two assholes pushed right through and I fell back into my living room. Rage and fear took over as they both came at me, I had no idea why they were there, but I assumed it was to kill me.

I jumped to my feet and got ready to fight for my life. My fists clenched tightly, ready for war. With all of my power and strength, I hit Bobby directly in the throat. A gasp escaped his mouth. He fell like a sack of rocks to the floor holding both hands around his throat, writhing in pain. Drew was on me fast and we wrestled, knocking a mirror and picture off of the wall. No one could get a punch in as we locked up like hockey players squaring off for a fight. Bobby was still laid out on the floor in what must have been incredible pain, trying to catch his breath. I could feel that I was stronger than Drew and was able to power him to the floor. Working my way to mount him, I was scared that Bobby was recovering enough to rejoin the fight. I knew I had limited time before I had to contend with two of them again. I had to end this, fast. Savagely I began to drive my fist into Drew's face while mounted on top of him. Every punch with a purpose of killing him, or knocking him out. After six or seven vicious hits, his head unable to absorb any more punishment, he went still.

I made my way toward Bobby and he put his hand up and said, "No more." I asked, "Who the fuck are you guys?" The name "Betty" came out of his mouth and I was sickened. He said they knew Betty and instantly I knew they had no clue to any real truth. I stopped him from saying any more and simply said, "I know that my ex-wife can tell some pretty big lies, so I am going to assume that is what she has done for you two idiots to practically break down my door and try and kill me. Get your buddy and get the fuck out of here." He helped Drew get to his feet and they hobbled out of my apartment. About 20 minutes later, it hit me; I don't know why, but this finally got me to the point of letting the law know what was going on with the Beast. She almost got me killed this time and I didn't want another surprise at my door someday.

I got to the door and low and behold, the Beast was there, holding a .22 caliber pistol. My heart instantly started pounding as I thought she would just point and shoot. She began walking toward me, "We are gonna talk." Words I've heard over and over for years with this woman. She showed me that she had the gun, but didn't point it straight at me. I knew that eventually, I would have to make a move to get the gun away from her. She finally reached the point of really wanting me dead, why else would she bring a gun? If she couldn't have me she didn't want anyone else to. Backing up into the living room, she began talking about how I didn't understand her feelings and that I never gave us a real chance.

I waited for an opportunity to strike and finally, it came. She was close enough to me and she looked down at the gun in her hand. At that time I dove toward her wrist with both hands. I felt her wrist come into my hands and clamped down as tight as my grip could hold. We both fell to the floor as I kept the gun pointed away from my face or head. It was still in her hands, but I started prying her fingers off one at a time as I held her wrist with my other hand. Scared out of my mind that it was going to go off and hurt someone, maybe my neighbor, I worked hard to get it out of her hand. Finally I broke her grip and had the gun in my hand. Quickly, I scampered away from her. She started yelling for me to kill her, "Shoot me Mark; just shoot me!" Fuck, she wanted to do a murder-suicide on me. Absolutely stunned, it hit hard that the one person who had already inflicted so much damage and pain on me was so close to taking me out. It wasn't enough for her; she had to put me in the ground, too.

Making my way toward the phone, I told her I was calling the cops and that she might want to leave. For a minute, she hesitated, like she didn't believe I would actually call them, and honestly, I didn't blame her. She had controlled me with fear for so long without any consequences; why would I actually step up now? It was different this time. I picked up the phone and called the police. She walked out the door. I told the police that my ex-wife was harassing me and kept coming to my apartment uninvited and causing trouble. The police officer asked if they needed to send a car over and I told him that she had left. He asked me to come into the station to fill out a complaint. After all of these years of suffering, I was finally going to use the law to protect myself.

I still had Betty's .22 gun with me and wanted to get rid of it. Since my fingerprints were on it too, I didn't want to walk into a police station packing a gun. The best thing I could think of was to dispose of it in the Kentucky River, about 20 miles from my apartment. I made a quick trip to the Tyrone Bridge, which connects Lawrenceburg and Versailles. As soon as I reached the bridge I made sure there were no cars coming and tossed the gun over the side. I watched it all the way down, thinking of what could have happened had I not gotten it out of Betty's hands.

Making my way back to Lexington, I wasn't sure what I would say to the police. I knew for sure was that I was going to file some sort of complaint. It had been a long time coming and nobody deserved it more than Betty. It felt strange walking into the station; usually I was on the wrong side of the law, as far as they were concerned. Walking up to the window, I told the officer, "I'm here to file a complaint against my ex-wife." She simply said, "Take a seat; someone will be with you in a minute to take your complaint." God, it was so easy, is all I thought; no wonder Betty had done this to me so many times. You don't need anything to file a complaint on someone. It was my turn now. I sat down with Officer Jones and told him details on how often Betty called me, how many times she showed up unannounced and would not leave when requested. I explained to him about her barricading herself by laying against the doorway and not letting me leave. Shockingly, he believed me. He typed up his report and a copy was sent to the judge for an emergency protective order to be served on Betty to stay away from me and refrain from calling my phone. I couldn't bring myself to tell him about the gun or the two idiots that came breaking through my door. I know for a fact it wasn't their fault. I did want her to be warned.

They served papers on her the next day and informed her to not contact me anymore. Immediately, I got a phone call. "What the hell is this, Mark?" I didn't respond. "Are you serious? I can't believe you would do this to me!" I couldn't believe she was actually playing the victim in all of this, but then again, this was the Beast. Finally, after letting her go off for a while, I told her that she was breaking the restraining order and that I would report her if she contacted me again. If something needed to be arranged with Jasmine, I would call her; otherwise, don't contact me again.

"Betty, I would love to put you through just a tiny bit of the hell you put me through these last few years; please, give me a reason to go back to the police. I'd love to get custody of Jasmine while your dumbass is on trial. I've got your gun and I will turn it over to the police and I promise you will go to jail for a long, long time, just try me you crazy bitch! You know you actually deserve to be in prison for what you have put me through all of these years."

Betty let out the most god-awful shriek I've ever heard

in my life and slammed the phone down on me. After all this time, and all of this pain, I never directly heard from her again.

A few months later I heard through the grapevine that Betty had finally met someone and had a boyfriend. After a year went by, my daughter told me that her mommy was getting married. I felt like I won the lottery! I walked around on cloud nine; I jumped up and down and danced for what felt like forever. I actually knew the nightmare was over and that she had moved on. It was more liberating than anything I've experienced in my entire life. Les was her fiancée's name; he was my best friend and didn't even know it. I went around telling everyone that I had a new best friend and just couldn't believe anyone would be crazy enough to get together with Betty. He was my savior.

The big day finally arrived and I smiled all day long knowing that she was getting married. A huge weight and burden lifted off my shoulders, finally.

As Betty and Les walked down the aisle, lovingly looking into each other's eyes, they exchanged vows. It was special and a day I will never forget, although I wasn't even there. I felt as if the memories of all the shit she had put me through finally were being put to bed. That night I experienced my first restful night of sleep in the past ten years.

Big surprise, Betty happened to be four months pregnant that special wedding day. She got her second victim! Les and Betty went on to have three more children; she wanted to make damn sure he couldn't leave, no matter how crazy she became. Hang in there, Les!

Made in the USA
Lexington, KY
30 October 2019